Invaders from Outer Space

Emily is having an asthma attack, Sam thought, and he began to feel panicky. He tried to calm down and think clearly. He had to try to get a note to this team—whoever they were. So far they seemed to be his and Emily's only hope.

Sam finished writing the note to the team, then sank back in his wheelchair. He didn't see Ghostwriter zip across the page and carry his message off into the future.

His eyes were fixed instead on the radio, from which a man's voice was broadcasting more terrifying news.

The strange creatures who had landed in New Jersey were definitely part of an invading army from Mars, the announcer said. An army that had attacked Grovers Mill and was about to attack the rest of the United States.

JOIN THE TEAM

Do you watch GHOSTWRITER on TV? Then you know that when you read and write to solve a mystery or unravel a puzzle, you're using the same smarts and skills the Ghostwriter Team uses.

We hope you'll join the team and read along to help solve the mysterious and puzzling goings-on in all of the GHOSTWRITER books!

Alien Alert

by Susan Korman

illustrated by Dan Krovatin

A Children's Television Workshop Book

BANTAM BOOKS
New York Toronto London
Sydney Auckland

ALIEN ALERT

A Bantam Book / September 1996

Ghostwriter *is a registered trademark of Children's Television Workshop.*
Ghostwriter™ and ●™ are
trademarks of Children's Television Workshop.
All rights reserved. Used under authorization.

Written by Susan Korman
Cover design by Marietta Anastassatos
Cover art of War of the Worlds: *Bettmann Archives*

The money that Children's Television Workshop earns when
you buy Ghostwriter books is put right back into CTW
educational projects. Thanks for helping!

ISBN 0-553-48410-9

Published simultaneously in the United States and Canada

Bantam Books are published by Bantam Books, a division of
Bantam Doubleday Dell Publishing Group, Inc. Its trademark,
consisting of the words "Bantam Books" and the portrayal of a
rooster, is Registered in U.S. Patent and Trademark Office and
in other countries. Marca Registrada. Bantam Books, 1540
Broadway, New York, New York 10036.

PRINTED IN THE UNITED STATES OF AMERICA

OPM   0 9 8 7 6 5 4 3 2 1

To Ann Bohan
with gratitude

chapter one

October 30, 1938

The silver spaceship landed in an open field. Harry Hall watched in horror as the hatch swung open. Out stepped the strangest-looking creature he had ever seen—a gigantic monster with black tentacles for arms. The alien's red eyes burned through the darkness like hot coals.

Harry stood frozen as the hideous creature from outer space stepped closer and closer, reaching for him with its terrible hairy fingers. . . .

"*Another* science fiction novel, Sam?"

Sam Gardella looked up from the book that lay open on his lap and grinned at his mother. She was standing in the doorway of his room, one hand behind her back.

"Eddie Ralff lent this one to me," Sam said.

"It's called *Creatures from Outer Space,* and it's really scary. These weird aliens attack this fellow—"

"You can spare me the gruesome details—I get the picture." Mrs. Gardella laughed as she came into the room and sat down on Sam's bed. "Are you sure you'll be okay tonight, honey?"

"I'll be fine, Mom," Sam reassured her. "Emily's coming over at eight—remember? It's not as if I'm going to be alone."

"I'm sorry I have to go to work," Mrs. Gardella went on. "But Frank really needs me when our customers are sick. We can't expect them to wait for their medicine." She brushed a strand of Sam's brown hair out of his eyes. "Even if we've had a crisis here."

Sam and his mother both glanced down at the heavy casts covering both his legs.

"The doctor says it'll only be another few weeks till these casts come off, Mom," he said softly. "I'm sorry you've had to stay home so much. I know—"

"Don't say another word." His mother cut him off. "You're my only child, Sam. I love taking care of you." Mrs. Gardella changed the subject by holding out the package she'd been hiding from Sam's view. It was wrapped in plain brown paper and tied with a pale-blue ribbon. "Here. This is for you."

Eagerly Sam ripped open the package. It contained a small, leather-bound book. "Thanks, Mom," he said, trying to sound enthusiastic. "It's a journal."

"It may not be your idea of a real present," Mrs. Gardella said. "But I thought you might like to do a little writing while you're stuck inside. You know your teacher thinks you show promise as a writer, Sam." Her blue eyes twinkled merrily. "As long as your spelling improves, that is."

"What am I going to write about?" Sam grumbled. He knew he sounded grouchy, but he couldn't help it. Ever since he'd broken his legs while he was horseback riding, he'd been bored stiff. "Nothing interesting is going to happen to me until I get out of this wheelchair and get these stupid casts off my legs."

"I'm sure you'll come up with something," Mrs. Gardella said as she bent over to kiss him. "I'll call you from the store. Don't forget to tell Emily that I'll bring her asthma medicine home."

"Okay," Sam said.

Mrs. Gardella hurried from the room. A few minutes later, Sam heard the front door slam and the car start up outside. He knew his mother was worried about leaving him tonight, but he and Emily would manage fine. He was twelve years old—old enough to take care of himself for a few hours.

Sam stared down at the small leather book his mother had given him. He ran his fingers over the word *Journal,* which was lettered in gold on the cover. Then he opened the book and gazed at the blank pages.

It's only seven o'clock, he thought. *I've got another hour till Emily comes over to listen to the radio.*

Using both arms, he wheeled his chair into the living room so that he could use the desk. He rummaged around in the drawer for a pen, then began to write.

October 30

Mom says she thinks it's time for me to start writing about my own life. I guess she forgot that nothing interesting is going to happen to me until I get out of this stupid wheelchair. With two b̶r̶o̶c̶k̶e̶n̶ broken legs, I can't do anything—I can't even go out trick-or-treating on Haloween tomorrow!

Tonight is Mom's first night back at work since I fell off Eddie Ralff's horse. When she drove away, I knew she felt bad, but she had to help Frank Connor, the fellow who works for her. Ever since Dad died, the store is all her resp̶o̶s̶bility responsibility. It's really hard for her sometimes.

My cousin Emily is coming over soon. Her favorite program is Bergen & McCarthy. *My favorite program is* Mercury Theatre. *I'm not sure which program we'll turn on tonight, but I sure hope it doesn't get interrupted. Lately there have been a lot of news updates. According to the newspapers and the presadent, the situation in Czechoslovakia (I looked up the spelling of this one in my geography book!) and the rest of Europe is getting worse, and ~~Mr~~ A.H. is making a lot of trouble.*

My father always used to say, "You're not the only pebble on the beach, Sam Gardella, and Grovers Mill, New Jersey, isn't the only town in the world." I know he'd think I was selfish, but I really hope tonight's show does NOT get interrupted by news about a possible war in Europe. It'll ruin everything!

So long.

Sam

"Hey, Sam!" Emily's voice rang through the quiet house.

Startled, Sam nearly dropped his pen. Was it almost eight o'clock already? He hated to admit it, but his mother was right. Writing in the journal had made the time fly.

A few seconds later, his eleven-year-old cousin, Emily, burst into the room, carrying an overnight bag. Her long brown hair hung down her back in two braids, and her blue eyes were sparkling.

"I'm sorry we're late," she said. "My parents were taking so long to get ready." She paused to catch her breath. "They're going to this dinner dance in New York City tonight, and my mother

5

had to put on her makeup, fix her hair, and then file her nails. It was unbelievable! You would think she was getting ready to meet Eleanor Roosevelt or something."

"I heard that, Emily Costello." Sam's aunt Mary stuck her head in the living room door. "Hi, Sam," she said. "Can I get you anything before we go?"

Sam shook his head. "I'm fine. Thanks, Aunt Mary. Mom wanted me to tell you that she's bringing home Emily's asthma medicine."

"Good," Aunt Mary said. "I forgot to pack her medicine for tonight, but she'll be coming back home tomorrow. Besides," she added, "Emily hasn't had a spell of asthma for quite some time."

Aunt Mary kissed Sam on the head and gave Emily a hug, then headed for the door. "Have fun, you two. We'll pick you up tomorrow afternoon, Emily."

"It's after eight, Emily," Sam said. "Turn on the radio."

"What do you want to listen to tonight?" she asked. "It's your turn to choose, Sam."

"How about *Mercury Theatre?*"

"Sure." Emily ran over and flicked on the radio. She twirled the dial, looking for the CBS station, which was broadcasting *Mercury Theatre*. She paused to listen to *The Edgar Bergen & Charlie McCarthy Show,* her favorite. As usual, the ventriloquist, Edgar Bergen, was joking with his dummy, Charlie McCarthy. "They're so funny," she said.

"Come on, Emily," Sam said impatiently. "We've already missed the beginning."

"Okay, here it is," Emily said a second later. She flopped onto the couch to listen.

Sam rolled the wheelchair closer to the radio—a large black appliance with a band across the top that read: Made with Pride in America by CRC, Continental Radio Company.

"I wonder what tonight's program is about, anyway," Emily said. "I didn't get a chance to check."

"The *Tribune's* over there." Sam pointed to the newspaper sitting on an end table. "You can— Hey . . ." A confused look crossed Sam's face as orchestra music filled the room. "This must be the wrong station, Emily. The announcer just said it's Ramon Raquello and His Orchestra."

"That's funny." Emily looked confused, too. She jumped up to check the dial. "I'm pretty sure I tuned in to the right station."

"Try moving the dial to the left a little," Sam suggested. "It's—"

"Shhh." Emily held up her hand as an announcer broke into the dance music. "Maybe they'll tell us what station this is."

"It's just another news update," Sam began. "Probably something else happened in Europe . . ."

Just then Sam noticed that Emily's eyes were open wide. As he listened, he discovered why. The news on the radio wasn't about Europe. It was about outer space!

". . . Ladies and gentlemen, we interrupt our program . . . to bring you a special bulletin. At twenty minutes before eight, Professor Farrell of the Mount Jennings Observatory, Chicago, Illinois, reported observing several explosions of incandescent gas, occurring at regular intervals on the planet Mars. . . ."

Emily looked at Sam as the dance music started up again.

"You're the space expert," she said. "What are they talking about?"

Sam shrugged. "I've never heard of anything like this. It must be pretty unusual. Otherwise, they wouldn't interrupt the show to make an announcement. It sounds really keen—I wish I could see it for myself."

The two cousins stayed glued to the radio as there was another interruption. This time a world-famous astronomer reported what he had seen through his telescope—the gas explosions from Mars were hurtling toward Earth at incredible speed.

A second later Sam sat bolt upright. "What? What'd he say?" He gestured for Emily to turn up the volume on the radio.

". . . a huge, flaming object, believed to be a

meterorite, fell on a farm in the neighborhood of Grovers Mill, New Jersey," the announcer said.

"Grovers Mill, New Jersey?" Emily gasped. "That thing landed right here?"

"Do you realize what this means, Emily?" Sam could feel his grin spreading from ear to ear. "It's incredible—a meteorite has practically landed in our own backyard!"

chapter two

The present, October 28

"Wait a minute, Gaby." Thirteen-year-old Alex Fernandez burst out laughing. "Let me get this straight. Two aliens with green skin and weird-looking eyes burst into Kevin Clarke's room last night and abducted him?"

Lenni Frazier, twelve, winked at Alex. "You've got it wrong, Alex," she said. "The aliens didn't take just Kevin. They also grabbed his brother, Malcolm."

"Oh, I see." Alex turned back to his little sister. "So, Gaby, did they take the family dog, too?"

Lenni and Tina Nguyen giggled. Gaby Fernandez could feel her face turning beet red. She and her friends were hanging out at Lenni's apartment, waiting for their Chinese food to arrive. And ever since she'd told everyone about

Kevin Clarke's UFO story, Alex had been teasing her.

"I'm just telling you what Kevin said, Alex," she snapped. "Besides, plenty of smart, normal people believe in UFOs. Maybe he's *not* making up the story."

Casey Austin had been listening carefully to the discussion. "A lot of people say they've been abducted by aliens," she said suddenly. "Grandma CeCe was telling me about that the other day in the supermarket. We saw a picture in the paper of a man who said he'd visited Pluto."

"Those dumb papers always make up stories like that, Casey," Gaby said. "I certainly wouldn't believe anything about UFOs that I read in one of them."

"So what about Kevin?" Tina asked Gaby. "Do you believe his story?"

Gaby hesitated. "I don't think so," she admitted. "But the way he told the story, it sounded so real. For a few minutes I did wonder about it."

Lenni looked amused. "What did he say, Gaby?" she asked.

"According to Kevin, the aliens took him and Malcolm on their spaceship and they had to lie down on a steel table to be X-rayed." Gaby blushed. As she told the team what Kevin had said, the words sounded silly, even to her own ears.

"X-rayed!" Alex hooted. "Kevin Clarke is such a liar! I can't believe he said that."

"Maybe he's trying to get attention or something," nine-year-old Hector Carrero put in. "My mom showed me an article that was in the paper last week. The article said that his parents got separated last year and lately his father has been threatening to take the two kids away from their mother."

"I read that story, too," Tina said, nodding. "It made things sound pretty nasty."

"It must be tough having Sparks Clarke for a father," Gaby added thoughtfully. "He was a big basketball star and everything, but I've heard he's not much of a dad."

"Just because his parents are having trouble, that doesn't mean Kevin would make up a wild story," Casey said.

"That's true, Casey," Gaby agreed, thinking of Casey's own situation. Right now she was living with her cousin, Jamal Jenkins, and his family, because of her mother's drinking problem. Casey was only eight, but she already knew a lot about family problems.

"I guess UFOs and aliens could really exist," Lenni said. "But I have to admit I'm pretty skeptical of these people who claim to have been *abducted* by UFOs. Especially when one of them is Kevin Clarke."

"Right," Alex agreed. "It's too weird to believe."

"What about Ghostwriter?" Gaby demanded. "You used to say that there was no such thing as ghosts—but then we met Ghostwriter."

"Uh . . . well . . ."

"Gotcha." A satisfied smile spread across Gaby's face. Gaby was right, and Alex knew it. None of them had believed in ghosts before they had met Ghostwriter and then formed the Ghostwriter Team.

Ghostwriter was an invisible friend who communicated with Gaby and the others by writing to them. None of them knew who he was or where he'd come from. All they knew was that he was their friend and he'd helped them solve lots of mysteries.

"Ghostwriter is different, Gaby," Alex said finally. "Ghostwriter is . . . well, he's Ghostwriter. We know he exists because he talks to us. Kevin hasn't shown you any proof that the alien abduction really happened."

"Sometimes you don't need proof," Gaby said. "Some things in life are just plain mysterious."

"Like why you'd believe Kevin Clarke for more than a second!" Alex said.

Gaby's eyes flashed. "Oh yeah, Alex? Well—"

Abruptly Lenni held up her hand. "Chill, you guys," she said. "I didn't invite you over for Chinese food so that we could argue about UFOs and aliens. You're supposed to be keeping me company while my dad works—okay?"

"Sorry, Lenni," Gaby said sheepishly. Gaby hadn't meant to start arguing with Alex in front of their friends. It was just that her big brother got her so mad sometimes. "Where's Jamal?" she asked. "Isn't he coming?"

Lenni nodded. "He said he'd be here by now. Maybe he got hung up at school."

Just then the doorbell rang.

"I bet that's our food," Lenni said.

Casey jumped to her feet. "I'll get it."

"Make sure it's not aliens coming to get you," Alex said with a chuckle.

The bell rang again.

"I'm coming, I'm coming," Casey murmured. A second later, she flung open the door.

"Your order's here, miss," the delivery person said in a muffled voice. He held out the cardboard box containing their food.

"Thank you," Casey said, her eyes on the box. As she was about to grasp the carton, she looked up, and her fingers froze.

The delivery person's face was grotesque. His huge nose and chin glowed in the dark corridor, and a pair of black, beady eyes peered out from under hairy eyebrows. His mouth was twisted into a terrible expression.

Casey screamed and backed away from the door. When she tried to speak, no words came out. Instead all she heard was her friends' laughter ringing out behind her.

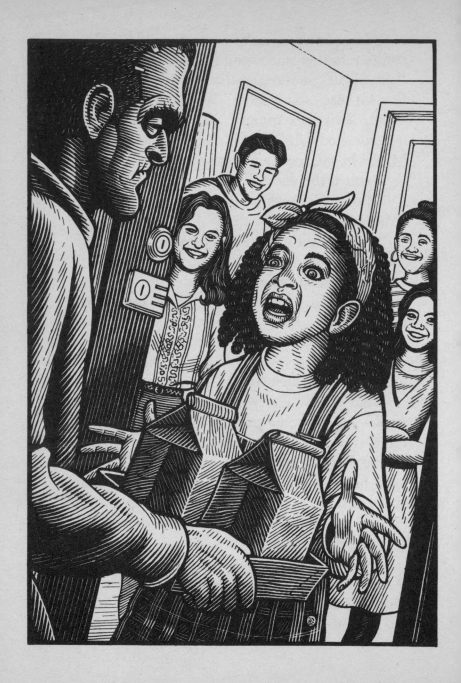

Suddenly the monster whipped off his rubber mask with a flourish.

"Jamal!" Casey exclaimed. "You scared me. How could you do a thing like that?"

Jamal grinned. "It was easy, little cousin. I bumped into the delivery girl outside and talked her into letting me bring the food up to you guys. She said it was fine since Lenni's dad had already paid." Jamal reached out to pat his cousin on the head, then hoisted the box onto his shoulder and strode into the loft. "Egg rolls here! Get your nice warm egg rolls here!"

Gaby watched Casey walk back inside Lenni's apartment. She could tell that Casey was still a little shaken. "Come over here, Casey," she called out. "Sit next to me."

"Nice costume, Jamal," Alex said. "You're a little early for Halloween, though."

"Not really," Jamal replied. "It's only a couple of days till the community center party, so I thought I'd try out my costume on you guys first."

Lenni grinned. "Trust me—it's a great costume. You'll definitely terrify the kids."

"I can't wait," Jamal said, smiling back.

All the team members were looking forward to the Haunted Halloween Party at the community center. They had volunteered to help out at the event, which was being held to raise money for a summer recreation program.

Lenni began dishing out servings of sesame noodles, white rice, and egg rolls. Gaby took a plate and passed it to Casey. Then she grabbed one for herself and sat down cross-legged next to Jamal's cousin. "What are you going to be for Halloween, Casey?" she asked.

"A clown," Casey replied.

Gaby smiled. Casey loved to fool around and play practical jokes. A clown suit was the perfect costume for her.

"How about you, Gaby?" Casey asked. "What are you going to be?"

"A witch," Gaby told her, before biting into an egg roll.

"That way she won't have to get dressed up or anything," Alex added.

"Very funny," Gaby commented. "At least I'm not the one who has to be a vampire because of my pointy fangs."

For once Alex didn't bother to reply.

Tina plucked up a sesame noodle with her chopsticks. "Kevin Clarke volunteered to help out at the party, too, didn't he?"

Lenni nodded. "Yeah, but Hank Delaney and Tamara Battle—they're the adults in charge of planning the party—are really mad at him. Tamara asked Kevin to hand out flyers advertising the party, and he never did it. Gaby and I wound up doing it last weekend." She pointed to a flyer that was stuck to the refrigerator. "Sounds fun, doesn't it?"

Come One, Come All
to a Haunted Halloween Party

Spooky Ghost Stories!
A Terrifying Tour through the Center!
Tricks, Treats, and Other Chilling Surprises!

WHEN: October 30, 7:30 P.M.
WHERE: Fort Greene Community Center
COST: $2 per ghost or goblin

*Proceeds will be donated to the Community Center's
Summer Recreation Program.*

"I think it sounds awesome," Casey said.

"And it's for a good cause," Tina reminded them.

"A *great* cause," Lenni corrected her. "This neighborhood could really use a summer program."

The team finished eating and then pitched in to clean up. When all the dishes had been washed and dried, Lenni handed out fortune cookies.

Alex was the first to crack his open. " 'Kindness has its own rewards,' " he read.

"Especially when you're kind to your sister," Gaby said with a laugh. "What does yours say, Casey?"

" 'Hold your head high and you will reach great heights,' " Casey replied. She laughed. "The person who makes fortune cookies must know I'm the youngest—and the shortest—kid on the team."

Jamal was next. "I'm not sure if mine is good or bad. 'You will get what you deserve.' "

"Sounds scary to me," Tina said. She read her fortune, followed by Lenni and Hector.

"How about you, Gaby?" Lenni asked.

Gaby cracked open her cookie as the rest of the team watched. The thin strip of white paper fluttered to the ground, and she scooped it up.

She read the words on the paper, then looked up at her friends.

"Come on, Gaby," Alex urged. "Read it out loud."

When she said the words aloud, a chill went up her spine.

" 'Things are not what they seem.' "

chapter three

October 30, 1938

"This is so keen, Emily," Sam said as the radio program switched back to the Meridien Room in the Hotel Park Plaza, where Ramon Raquello and His Orchestra were performing. "I can't believe a meteorite has landed in Grovers Mill, New Jersey!"

"It's amazing," Emily agreed. A second later, a puzzled expression crossed her face. "What's a meteorite, anyway?" she asked.

"It's matter from the solar system," Sam explained. "I read a whole book about meteors. The matter becomes a meteor*ite* when it reaches the surface of the earth without being completely vaporized."

"Wait a minute, Sam." Emily pointed to the radio. "Now they're talking to someone from Grovers Mill." She frowned. "It sounded like his name is Mr. Wilmuth. Do you know anyone named Wilmuth?"

Sam shook his head and motioned for his cousin to be quiet. He didn't want to miss a word of the broadcast.

The announcer, Carl Phillips, said he'd just arrived in Grovers Mill and was standing with a Mr. Wilmuth in a field on his farm. As the two men studied the object that had fallen to Earth, the announcer's voice grew more and more excited.

"I guess that's the . . . *thing,* directly in front of me, half buried in a vast pit. . . . What I can see of the . . . object itself doesn't look very much like a meteor. . . . It looks more like a huge cylinder."

Sam and Emily exchanged glances. A huge cylinder? Carl Phillips went on to describe it as metal, with a yellowish white sheen. He said curious spectators were gathering at the scene.

"I wish I could go take a look for myself," Sam said, pounding the arm of his wheelchair in frustration. "My one chance to get close to something from outer space and I'm trapped in this stupid chair."

"How would we find it, anyway?" Emily asked. "They say this thing fell in Grovers Mill, but neither of us has ever heard of the Wilmuth farm."

"The announcer said there are lots of people surrounding the cylinder," Sam said. "I'm sure we could track it down."

His attention was brought back to the radio by a change in the announcer's voice. Carl Phillips was talking faster and louder as he got more and more excited. He described how the police had arrived on the scene and now hundreds of people were staring into the pit where the cylinder had landed.

A low humming noise came from the radio.

"Do you hear that, Sam?" Emily asked. "What's that weird sound?"

"Got me." Sam shrugged. His eyes grew wide at the announcer's next words.

"Just a minute!" Carl Phillips exclaimed. "Ladies and gentlemen, this is the most terrifying thing I have ever witnessed. . . . Someone's *crawling out of the hollow top.* Someone or something. I can see peering out of that black hole two luminous disks. . . . Are they eyes? It might be a face."

"Someone's crawling out of the cylinder?" Emily gasped. "What's going on, Sam?"

Sam rolled himself over to his desk to scoop up the journal he'd been writing in before Emily showed up. "I don't know," he told his cousin. "But I have a feeling we're listening to something really big and important. I want to write down everything that's happening."

Emily stared at him in disbelief. "You're going to write? At a time like this?"

"That's exactly what I'm going to do," Sam told her. "Mom gave me a journal so that I could write about my life. And this is the most incredible thing that's ever happened to me—or Grovers Mill."

The sound of terrified voices filled the air as Sam reached for his pen and began to record the events that were happening in his hometown. He wrote under the entry he'd started earlier:

8 P.M., October 30
This is incredible. Something has landed in Grovers Mill, New Jersey! At first the scientists thought it was a meteor, now they think it's an extXatere object from outer space. It sounds like it's very big and it's shaped like a metal cylinder. According to the newscaster, the object has landed on the Wilmuth farm and hundreds of people—including the New Jersey Militia— have gathered in Grovers Mill to see it. I wish Emily and I could go too, but we can't, on account of my being in a wheelchair. Emily and I don't know where the Wilmuth farm is, but it must be pretty close. Grovers Mill is a small town. It's just Emily and me here at home to-night. . . .

Sam looked up. His cousin had grown completely silent as the announcer continued to describe the scene on the Wilmuth farm. Now Emily's eyes were wide with fright.

"Good heavens," the announcer gasped. "Something's wriggling out of the shadow like a gray snake. Now it's another one, and another one, and another one. They look like tentacles to me. There, I can see the thing's body. It's large as a bear and it glistens like wet leather. But that face. It—Ladies and gentlemen, it's indescribable. I can hardly force myself to keep looking at it, it's so awful."

Sam wrote as fast as he could, trying to get down the announcer's every word. From time to time, he glanced at Emily. She still looked scared stiff.

"Oh, Sam," she said a few minutes later, as piano music started up. "What are we going to do?"

"It's okay, Emily." Sam tried to reassure his cousin in a calm voice. "We just have to wait and see what happens. The police are on the scene, and so is the New Jersey Militia—whatever that is. I'm sure we're safe."

"But what if—"

"Don't worry," Sam said.

"I wish we weren't alone tonight," Emily murmured. She gazed out the window at the dark sky. "Maybe I should call somebody, or try to go for help or something."

Sam followed her gaze and looked out the window. Strange pulsing lights lit up the black sky.

What's going on? Sam wondered. *Are those lights coming from the Wilmuth farm?*

Suddenly the radio announcer gasped. The creatures from the cylinder had shot a huge fireball at the crowd, blasting a group of men standing nearby. Now woods, barns, and cars were all burning like wildfire.

"It's coming this way!" the announcer cried. "About twenty yards to my right . . ."

Sam gasped as Carl Phillips screamed in horror at the approaching fireball. A second later, the announcer's words trailed off. Then came the sound of the microphone crashing to the ground.

Emily covered her face in her hands. "Turn it off, Sam!" she shouted. "I don't want to listen anymore."

"It'll be okay, Emily," Sam said. He knew his words didn't sound convincing, but he didn't know what else to say. He picked up the pen and began to write again:

We don't know what's going on or what's going to happen to us, but Emily and I are here all alone. We may be in big trouble. . . .

Across the room, Emily was taking great heaving breaths as she tried to stay calm.

Sam stopped writing for a second. He couldn't believe it. Aliens had landed right here in Grovers Mill. He stared at the page, thinking about the horrible scene at the Wilmuth farm. It seemed as if

27

the whole town—and maybe the whole world—was in terrible danger.

Sam was so worried, he didn't even notice as the letters on the page of his journal began to rearrange themselves.

What on earth were he and Emily going to do?

chapter four

The present, October 29

Gaby chewed the end of her pencil and looked up at the blackboard where her English teacher had written the assignment. She knew Ms. Ramirez *thought* she was being clever, coming up with a Halloween assignment, but in Gaby's opinion the idea was a little silly.

She reread the teacher's directions:

WRITE TWO SENTENCES ABOUT SOMETHING WEIRD OR SPOOKY THAT HAPPENED TO YOU. ONE OF THESE SHOULD BE BASED ON FACT. THE OTHER ONE SHOULD BE BASED ON FICTION. IN OTHER WORDS, MAKE UP SOMETHING AND TRY TO TRICK US INTO THINKING IT'S TRUE!

29

How about my parents won the lottery and I'm going to inherit a million dollars as soon as I turn eighteen? Gaby thought. She wrote down the sentence, then stared at it. *Nope,* she decided a minute later, *it's not scary or weird enough.*

She scratched that, then started again. "My brother Alex is from Transylvania; that's why he hates garlic and sleeps in a coffin."

Better, she thought.

Suddenly the words in her notebook began to glow.

Hi, Gaby. Need some help?

Gaby quickly wrote back. "Hi, Ghostwriter. Boy, am I glad to see you. I can't think of anything to write."

Don't worry. That happens to the best writers. You just need one good idea.

"Two good ideas," Gaby corrected him. "Ms. Ramirez wants us to come up with two sentences."

Ghostwriter zipped over to the board to read the assignment, then returned in a flash.

I like your sentence about Alex, he wrote, but it's not very convincing. I think you can do better than that.

"Any ideas?" Gaby asked.

Why don't you think about the last twenty-four hours, Ghostwriter suggested. Maybe something weird happened to you that you've forgotten about.

"Thanks, Ghostwriter," Gaby wrote back. "I'll give it a try."

As Ghostwriter faded away, Gaby thought about the past twenty-four hours. Not much had happened. She'd gone to school, then had Chinese food with the team at Lenni's.

Hmmm . . . Chinese food. An idea suddenly came to her. She quickly scribbled down her thoughts and was finishing up when the teacher called out, "Time's up, class."

"Already?" Sara Hipple groaned.

Two seats away, Gaby saw Kevin Clarke put down his pencil. A smirk flickered across his face.

"Okay, everybody," Ms. Ramirez said. "Listen up. We're going to play a little game. I'm going to go around the room and ask you to read your two sentences. Then your classmates are going to guess which one is true and which one is false."

Levar Mott waved his hand in the air. "What's the point of this, Ms. Ramirez?" he asked.

The English teacher smiled. "You'll see, Levar."

Sara Hipple went first. Gaby thought it was easy to guess which sentence she'd made up. Sara claimed she'd been to a rock concert the night before and been kissed by the drummer.

"No way!" Joey Hurston shouted out.

Everyone else agreed.

Sara grinned. "I guess I wasn't very convincing."

Melissa Gao was next. Gaby thought Melissa's sentences were a lot more clever. Gaby had trouble finding the false one, and so did the rest of the class.

31

"Sentence one," Melissa said, then read. "Last night three lightbulbs in our house went out at the exact same time, and my grandmother believes it was because of a ghost.

"I had a dream that my cousin Lee called, and the next day, he really did."

There was silence for a few minutes as the class tried to guess which sentence was false. Finally Gaby raised her hand. "Sentence number two," she said.

Melissa grinned and shook her head. "I made up the first one."

Ms. Ramirez looked pleased. "Melissa has helped to prove my point, class. Her very specific details, such as 'three lightbulbs,' are what helped convince us. Isn't that true?"

Gaby thought about it for a second, then nodded.

"That's what I'd like to see you work into your stories," the teacher went on. "Details that give your stories the ring of truth, even if they're made up."

"Hey, Ms. Ramirez!" Levar's hand shot up again. "Do you think this will help me with my dad?"

"What do you mean, Levar?" the teacher asked.

Levar grinned. "Now I know how to lie better. I'll be able to make up great excuses when I come home late."

"That wasn't what I had in mind," Ms. Ramirez said dryly. "But I'm glad you get the point."

One by one, the class continued reading their sentences aloud. Finally the teacher came to Kevin Clarke.

Gaby's ears perked up as he began to read.

"Sentence number one: Two nights ago, a UFO landed on the roof of my building and abducted me and my little brother, Malcolm."

He paused. "Sentence number two: Last year my father took our whole family to Africa on safari."

"Sentence number one is the lie!" yelled a boy from the front row.

"Right," Melissa Gao agreed. "The second sentence isn't even about something weird or spooky."

"What about the rest of you?" asked Ms. Ramirez. "What do you think?"

The rest of the class quickly agreed that Kevin had made up the first sentence. Gaby readily went along with everyone else. Yesterday she'd believed Kevin's UFO story for a few seconds, but today his lie stuck right out.

Everyone looked at Kevin expectantly. The smirk Gaby had seen earlier crossed his face again.

"You're all wrong," he said. "I made up the second sentence."

Ms. Ramirez cocked her head. "Come on now, Kevin. You don't really expect us to believe that a UFO landed on the roof of your building, do you?"

"I don't care what you believe," he muttered, turning away from the teacher.

Gaby watched Kevin closely, startled by his reaction. Did he really believe the alien story? He must, she reasoned; otherwise he wouldn't get so angry when no one else believed it.

On the other hand, the sentence about the safari sounded made up, too. After hearing about Kevin's parents, it seemed unlikely that Sparks Clarke would take the whole family on a trip.

Maybe Kevin made up both sentences, Gaby decided.

"Thank you, Kevin," Ms. Ramirez said finally, and called on Gaby.

Thoughts of Kevin fled Gaby's mind as she turned back to her notebook, where she'd written her sentences. She couldn't help feeling pleased with them.

"Sentence number one," she said. "I have a very good friend who's a ghost.

"Sentence number two: Last night I had a fortune cookie and the fortune was, 'Beware of Halloween. Something spooky is going to happen to you.' "

Ms. Ramirez gave a mock shiver. "Oooh, that does sound eerie. What do you think, class?"

"That one's easy, too," Sara Hipple called out. "Gaby made up sentence number one. She doesn't have a friend who's a ghost."

The rest of the class nodded their agreement.

"Right," Gaby lied. She quickly looked down to hide both her smile and her secret. She'd played with the truth a little, but so what?

That was exactly what the assignment was about.

chapter five

"**W**ait up, Casey!" Gaby called out later that afternoon. She was a block away from the community center when she spotted her friend. The team was meeting Tamara Battle at the center to talk about tomorrow's Haunted Halloween Party.

"Hi, Gaby!" Casey turned around and waited for Gaby to catch up.

"You're a little late, too," Gaby remarked. "I bet everybody else is already at the center."

"I just came from the library," Casey said. "I've been doing some research on UFOs and I found out all kinds of interesting information."

Gaby raised her eyebrows. "Do yourself a favor and don't tell Alex. You'll never hear the end of it."

Casey nodded. "I know. But after reading this

stuff, I'm more positive than ever that UFOs exist." Her voice grew more and more excited as she told Gaby some of the things she'd learned. "Most of the people who've been abducted describe the same thing: They say that the aliens come for them and take them on their ship and do X rays and stuff, just like Kevin Clarke said. And a lot of them talk about how the aliens can read their minds."

"Really?" Gaby grinned. "It sounds like a *Twilight Zone* episode to me."

As the two girls entered the Fort Greene Community Center, the sound of hip-hop music filled the air. It was coming from a large portable stereo on the floor in the main room of the center.

Casey was about to tell Gaby more about what she'd read when Tamara Battle whipped past them, carrying a legal pad. "Hi, Gaby, Casey!" Tamara flashed the two girls a warm smile. She was wearing a black skirt and an oversized blouse printed with bright African patterns. A pencil stuck out from behind one ear. "Thanks for coming. I've got a lot to do for the party and need all the help I can get. You haven't seen Kevin Clarke, have you?"

Casey shook her head.

"He was in English this afternoon," Gaby said, "but I haven't seen him since then."

Tamara frowned. "I'm getting frustrated with that boy," she said. "I know everything's not right at home, but he promised to help, and now— Oh, never mind." Abruptly she changed the subject. "Let's just get started."

Gaby and Casey followed the older woman into a meeting room at the back of the center. The two girls waved to the other team members, who were already sitting around the table.

"Okay," Tamara began. "Hank Delaney and I are going to handle refreshments and getting the party organized. I need you guys to help me with the spooky tour."

"What's the spooky tour?" asked Hector.

Tamara grinned. "Basically we're going to lead the kids through the center and scare the daylights out of them," she explained. "After that we'll give everybody a snack and play games and tell ghost stories."

"Sounds cool," Jamal said.

"Definitely," Lenni agreed. "So what are we supposed to do?"

"That's what we're here to figure out," Tamara replied. "Here's a list of what needs to be done." She put her clipboard on the table and showed them a long list of jobs. "Why don't you guys figure out who's going to do what for the tour? I'll come back and check on you in a little while. If anybody needs me, I'll be out front helping Hank string up the jack-o'-lantern lights."

As Tamara left the room, Gaby scanned the list of jobs. "We've got a lot to do, guys," she said. "We need someone to peel grapes for the vat of monster eyeballs, cook spaghetti for guts, and—"

Casey's eyes jumped down to the bottom of the list. "I want to hand out the treats," she said.

"Okay," Gaby replied. "That's one job taken care of." She wrote Casey's name next to that item and began reading the others out loud. " 'Make monster eyeballs.' Who wants to do that?"

"Sounds fun." Tina grinned as she raised a hand. "I'll make them."

"I'll make the spaghetti for the human guts," Hector volunteered.

"Since I'm going to get dressed as a witch, I'll make the witch's brew," Gaby said.

Next they decided that Alex and Jamal would lead the spooky tour through the center in their costumes. Alex was going to be a vampire, and Jamal couldn't wait to put on his Frankenstein's monster costume again.

They had almost finished assigning jobs when Kevin Clarke stuck his head in the door. His little brother, Malcolm, was with him.

"What's up, guys?" Kevin said.

Gaby gave Malcolm a big smile. The cute five-year-old had huge brown eyes and dark hair shaved close to his head.

"You're a little late, Kevin," Tina said. "Didn't Tamara ask you to be here at four o'clock?"

Kevin shrugged. "That's the way it goes. Tamara

can't expect me to spend all my time on a Halloween party. I had other stuff to do after school."

Gaby watched as he sauntered into the room
and picked up the clipboard. He scanned the list,
then said, "Looks like you guys got it covered."

"No thanks to you," Alex muttered.

Kevin's head shot up. "Did you say something,
Alex?"

Alex crossed his arms and stared back at Kevin.
"I guess you were too busy traveling around outer
space to show up at the community center on
time. Is that it?"

Kevin glowered at Alex as he adjusted the visor
of his Chicago Bulls cap. "I said I had things to
do—okay?"

"Fine," Alex snapped. He wheeled back to
Gaby. "What's next?"

But Kevin wasn't finished. "Look, Fernandez.
You don't have to believe me about the UFO
stuff. It really doesn't matter. I know what the
truth is."

"Did you tell them about the aliens?" Malcolm
asked eagerly. "Did you tell them about the spaceship that came and landed on our roof?

"It was really cool," the little boy went on, turning to Alex and the rest of the team. "The aliens
took us on their ship, and they let me drive! Kevin
says—"

But Kevin cut him off. "I'm not even going to
show up for the Halloween party," he went on. "I

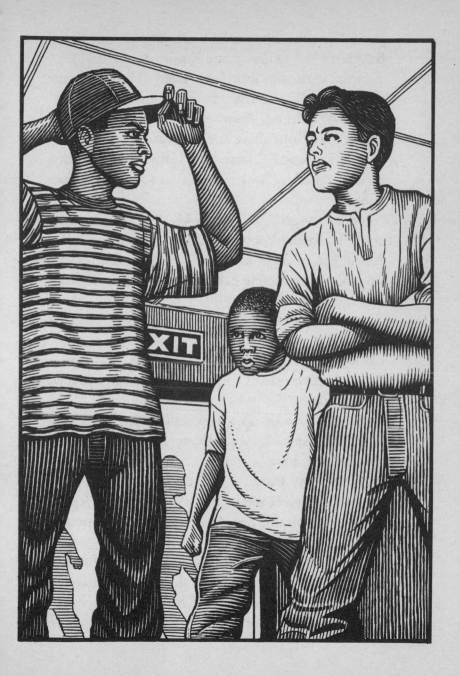

came down here to tell Tamara that my father got tickets to the Lakers game tomorrow night."

Jamal looked at him, surprised. "The Lakers are playing the Knicks tomorrow night in New York?"

Kevin smirked. "No, they're playing in L.A. We're flying out there for the season opener."

"No kidding," Jamal said. Gaby could tell that he didn't believe a word of Kevin's story. "Sounds cool."

"That's right," Kevin told him. "It's totally cool. My father knows a lot of people in the NBA. All he has to do is ask, and"—Kevin snapped his fingers—"presto. He can get tickets to any game, just like that."

At the other end of the table, Lenni rolled her eyes.

"We've got great seats," Kevin continued. "Right next to Jack O'Rourke. I bet you guys have heard of him."

Casey's eyes lit up. "Jack O'Rourke?" she echoed. "The star of *Beach Bums?* Are you really sitting next to him?"

"Front-row seats," Kevin declared.

"Maybe you'll see us on TV," Malcolm added. "My dad says the people sitting in the front row always get to be on TV."

"Come on, my main man." Kevin put his arm around Malcolm. "We'll catch you people later." He laughed loudly. "Happy Halloween."

Gaby watched Kevin go.

"That guy is such a jerk," Alex said. He shook his head in disgust. "How stupid does he think we are?"

"I can't believe he's going to meet Jack O'Rourke," Casey said. "That guy is like the biggest star on TV. Kevin and Malcolm are *so-o-o* lucky."

"That's what Kevin *said,* Casey," Gaby began. "But I don't think—"

"Maybe he's telling the truth, Gaby," Casey cut in. "Why would he make up a story like that?"

"He's a liar, Casey," Jamal said softly. "As far as I can see, the guy never tells the truth about anything."

"Remember that family tree project?" Lenni asked Gaby. She smiled and shook her head as she told Casey about what had happened. "When Gaby's class made family trees last year, Kevin claimed he was related to Frederick Douglass on his mother's side and Martin Luther King, Jr., on the other!"

"He's very creative," Tina said as everyone but Casey laughed.

Casey's face flushed. "Well, I believe him about the UFOs *and* the Lakers game," she said stubbornly.

Gaby was about to say something else, then decided to stay quiet. *So what if Casey believes him?* she thought. For some reason Casey needed to believe that Kevin was telling the truth. Maybe it had something to do with Casey's own family situation, Gaby decided. Casey's mother hadn't been very reliable while she was drinking, and that had hurt Casey. Maybe Casey didn't want Kevin to be hurt the same way by his father.

As Gaby turned back to the checklist, she found herself hoping that Kevin was telling the truth, too—at least about the basketball game. Judging by the look on Malcolm's face, the little boy was going to be very disappointed if he didn't get to go to L.A. with his dad.

October 30, 1938

Sam stopped writing in his journal for a second and stared at the radio. His fear was growing by the minute. Emily sat nearby on the couch, nervously listening to every word as the radio broadcast from the Wilmuth farm continued. Every so often Sam heard her wheeze. He hoped her asthma wasn't about to kick in.

According to one of the new announcers, at least forty people in Grovers Mill, including Carl Phillips and six state troopers, had been burned to death by the creatures inside the crater.

Sam shuddered as the announcer said their bodies were "charred beyond recognition." Sam had read a lot of science fiction, but never, in all his wildest dreams, had he imagined that something like this could really happen. And in Grovers Mill! Until today, Sam had considered Grovers Mill, New Jersey, one of the most boring places in the world.

He glanced over at his cousin. "Do you think . . . ," he began. He swallowed, then tried again. "I mean, I wonder if anyone we know died."

"Don't think like that, Sam," Emily said abruptly.

Sam nodded, but his thoughts flew anyway to his mother at work. Their family's pharmacy was outside Grovers Mill, in Princeton Junction, New Jersey. Was his mother safe? Did she even know about the incredible events that were unfolding right here?

Sam glanced outside the window. The night seemed surprisingly quiet, given what was happening only a few miles away. In the distance he could make out a steady stream of headlights as cars flowed along the main road. According to the radio, the town was being evacuated. If only there were some way for him and Emily to find out if his mother was okay, then get out of here, too.

As if she were reading his mind, Emily spoke up suddenly. "I'm going to try to call your mother again, Sam. I want to make sure she's okay. She's probably worried about us, too."

Sam nodded. Emily had tried to reach his mother several times but couldn't get through.

Sam picked up his pen and continued to record the horrifying events as he listened to the reports coming in on the radio.

According to the broadcaster, the state militia was about to begin a full military operation against the strange creatures from the capsule.

Who would have guessed it? Sam wrote. *For the past few months, everyone had expected to hear about war in Europe, and now a different kind of war is happening right here in the United States.*

Sam could hear Emily in the kitchen slamming the phone down in frustration. "I still can't get through," she wailed. "The lines are jammed!"

"Wait a minute, then try again," Sam called back.

"Emily and I have tried to reach my mother by phone, but so far . . ."

Suddenly Sam dropped his pen. Something strange was happening in his journal! The letters were swirling and rearranging themselves as a glowing light danced across them.

Sam blinked hard. "What the heck . . . ?" His jaw dropped open as the letters spun into a message—a message that was addressed to him!

Hello, Sam.

Sam's eyes darted around the room. "Wh-Who are you?" he stammered.

My name is Ghostwriter, the letters spelled out across the page. I thought you might need some help.

"Wh-What's going on?" he demanded. "Emily!" he shouted loudly. "Come in here right away!"

You have to write to me. That's the only way we can talk to each other, Ghostwriter continued.

Emily hurried into the room. "What's wrong now?"

Sam lifted a finger and pointed weakly to his journal.

"What is it?" Emily rushed to his side and looked down at the page. "Is this some kind of joke?" she muttered. "I don't understand."

"I don't, either," Sam told her in a shaky voice. "First the capsule, and now . . ." He swallowed hard. "I'm scared, Emily."

Emily reached down and scooped up the pen.

"Are you really a ghost?" she scrawled across the page.

A second later came the reply.

Yes. I'm your friend. There's nothing to be afraid of.

Emily screamed and tossed the pen back on Sam's lap as if she'd been bitten by a wild creature. "You try, Sam," she said in a whisper.

Sam slowly picked up the pen again. "How can you help us?" he wrote. "Emily and I are stuck in the house until my mother comes home. We don't know what to do."

The glowing lights danced across the pages of Sam's journal as Ghostwriter reread Sam's description of what was happening a few miles away.

Things sound very dangerous. Perhaps the team can help.

"Who is the team?" wrote Sam.

My friends, Ghostwriter explained. **Their names are Lenni, Jamal, Alex, Gaby, Casey, Tina, and Hector. Tell them what's happening and they can try to help.**

"Okay," Sam replied. "Dear Team," he wrote. "Something terrible has happened in Grover's Mill . . ."

A sudden sound made him look up. Across the room, Emily was slumped on the couch, gasping for air. The color had drained from her face, and she was wheezing loudly as she struggled to breathe.

Emily is having an asthma attack, Sam thought, and he began to feel panicky. He tried to calm down and think clearly. He had to try to get a note to this team—whoever they were. So far they seemed to be his and Emily's only hope.

Sam finished writing the note to the team, then sank back in his chair. He didn't see Ghostwriter zip across the page and carry his message off into the future.

His eyes were fixed instead on the radio, from which a man's voice was broadcasting more terrifying news.

The strange creatures who had landed in New Jersey were definitely part of an invading army from Mars, the announcer said. An army that had attacked Grovers Mill, and was about to attack the rest of the United States.

chapter six

The present, October 30

"Did you bring the spaghetti, Hector?" Gaby asked.

It was nine o'clock on Saturday morning, and the team was back at the community center, trying to get organized for the Haunted Halloween Party that night.

Hector smiled and held up a big pot filled with cold spaghetti. "Mom and I cooked it last night. I can't wait to see those kids reach in to feel the stuff after I tell them it's human guts!"

"It'll gross them out." Lenni smiled with delight. "Wait till you see this." She reached into her backpack and pulled out an old black wig. "This can be a witch's scalp."

Tina pretended to shudder. "You guys have great ideas," she said. "How come you're so good at spooking people?"

"It's easy when your sister's a witch," Alex said. He slapped Gaby on the back.

"As usual, I'm not laughing at your lame joke, Alex," she replied.

"Here's my contribution." Jamal had a plastic bag filled with small, dried-up bones. "Grandma CeCe was making chicken soup and thought we could use these."

This time Casey shivered for real. "I'm glad she didn't give them to me. What are you going to do with those, Jamal?"

"I thought we could stick them in a jar and pretend they were the bones of a monster's victims," he said.

"Cool." Alex gave him a thumbs-up. "Have you seen all the decorations Tamara and Hank are putting up?"

"The center looks great," Casey said. She covered her mouth as she let out a big yawn. "I hope I can stay awake until the party starts."

"You were up all night again reading those UFO books," Jamal said. "I told you it was getting late."

"I couldn't help it," Casey replied. "They're so interesting."

Gaby smiled as Casey went on about UFOs. "You're becoming a walking UFO encyclopedia," Gaby said as she looked at the party list. She marked off *witch's brew*—she'd made a batch that morning. The next item was goody bags. Tamara and Casey were filling "hands" (otherwise known as surgical gloves) with candy and other surprises. "Are the hands finished, Casey? Did you . . ."

Gaby's voice trailed off as the words on the page began to swirl.

"Look," she said to Casey. "Ghostwriter's here. I think he wants to help with the party, too."

Hello, Team, Ghostwriter wrote. I'm glad I found you together. I need your help.

Alex grabbed the pen from the string around his neck and wrote back.

"What's up, Ghostwriter?"

Sam and Emily are in trouble, Ghostwriter began.

"Can you tell us more?" Alex asked.

Ghostwriter disappeared, then came back with a longer message.

Dear Team,

Something terrible has happened in Grovers Mill. Martains have invaded New Jersey and Emily and I are very frightened. Ghostwriter says you can help us. Is this true? Please help. We think we're in terrible danger. Thank you.

—Sam and Emily

"What are Martains?" Hector asked, pointing to the word.

"It must be *Martians,*" Jamal told him. "Somebody made a spelling mistake."

"Martians?" Lenni said, looking at the team. "Is Ghostwriter for real?"

Gaby prodded Alex with her elbow. "Ask him for more clues, Alex," she urged him.

"Ghostwriter, we need more information," Alex wrote.

Okay, Ghostwriter replied. Then he disappeared.

A few minutes later, the team was still staring at the paper, waiting for Ghostwriter to return.

"Is it my imagination, or is Ghostwriter taking a long time?" Lenni asked.

Jamal nodded. "It does seem like a while," he said.

Finally Ghostwriter glowed across the page again.

"This is some message," Alex said. "No wonder it took him so long."

"It looks like part of somebody's diary," Casey said. "It must belong to that boy Sam."

October 30
   Mom says she thinks it's time for me to start writing about my own life. I guess she forgot that nothing interesting is going to happen to me until I get out of this stupid wheelchair. With two b̶r̶ocken broken legs, I can't do anything—I can't even go . . .

Gaby's eyes quickly scanned the first few paragraphs. The diary entry didn't say much except that Sam had broken his legs and he was bored. She read on.

> . . . *Emily is coming over soon. Her favorite program is* Bergen & McCarthy. *My favorite program is* Mercury Theatre. *I'm not sure which program we'll turn on tonight, but I sure hope it doesn't get interrupted. Lately there have been a lot of news updates. According to the newspapers and the presadent, the situation in Czechoslovakia (I looked up the spelling of this one in my geography book!) and the rest of Europe is getting worse, and* ~~Ad~~ *A.H. is making a lot of trouble . . ."*

"Boy, this kid Sam is a terrible speller," Lenni remarked.

"I'll say," Jamal agreed. "Let's start a casebook."

Gaby nodded and flipped open her notebook to a blank page. "Okay, guys, what do we have so far?"

"Well, we know from Sam's diary that he lives in New Jersey in the town . . ." Jamal ran his finger over the diary entry. "Here it is, Grovers Mill."

"Sam has two broken legs, and he likes a show called *Mercury Theatre,*" added Tina.

"His cousin likes *Bergen & McCarthy* better," Lenni said.

As her friends called out clues, Gaby jotted everything down. A few minutes later, they looked at what they had:

CLUES

1. Sam and Emily are cousins who live in Grovers Mill, New Jersey.

2. They like two TV shows, Mercury Theatre and Bergen & McCarthy.

3. Sam has two broken legs.

4. There's a situation in Czechoslovakia and Europe. Bad guy (?) with the initials A̶X̶ A.H. is causing trouble.
   Questions: What is the situation in Europe?
   Who is A̶X̶ A.H.?
   Are Martians really invading New Jersey?????

While the others had called out clues, Alex had been sitting quietly. "This is so bizarre," he said finally. "I guess it's just a coincidence, but suddenly everybody seems to be talking about Martians and UFOs."

"It does seem weird," Jamal admitted. Then he shrugged. "Maybe this kid Sam is making up stories, too."

"I don't believe Kevin for one second," Lenni said firmly. "But I do believe what Ghostwriter says. If he says that these kids need our help, then they need our help."

"Right," Casey agreed. Then she added softly, "Maybe they're both telling the truth—Ghostwriter and Kevin."

"Does anybody have a newspaper?" Tina asked suddenly. She pointed to the date from Sam's journal. "That's today's date. Maybe there's something in the paper about Europe or this guy A.H."

"That's a great idea, Tina," Jamal said. "Let me see if I can find Tamara. She probably has a paper."

"Last I saw her, she and Hank were putting up spider decorations in the main room," Lenni told him.

Jamal nodded and hurried away.

"Has anybody heard of those TV shows?" Hector asked. "*Mercury Theatre* and *Bergen & McCarthy?*"

Gaby and the others shook their heads.

"That *is* strange," Gaby said, frowning. "These two kids live in New Jersey, which isn't very far from where we live in Brooklyn. So how come we've never heard of the shows?"

"Maybe they're on a local cable channel," Lenni suggested.

Jamal came back into the room, carrying a newspaper. "I've already checked the headlines," he began. "And there's nothing in here about a situation in Europe. The big story seems to be about a terrorist attack in the Middle East."

"What about the TV section?" Tina suggested. "Let's see if there's a listing for *Mercury Theatre* or *Bergen & McCarthy.*"

"Nothing," Alex said a minute later. He folded up the paper and tossed it onto the table. "That's a dead end."

"Well, we know that Sam lives in New Jersey, right?" Hector said. "All we have to do is find a kid named Sam with a cousin named Emily who lives in Grovers Mill."

"Hector," Tina groaned. "You make it sound so easy. Grovers Mill is miles away, plus we don't even know Sam's last name!"

There was a puzzled look on Jamal's face. "How could an army of Martians be invading New Jersey? It's like something from a science fiction book."

"Or a story from Kevin Clarke," Alex put in. "It doesn't make sense. Maybe Ghostwriter is playing a Halloween trick on us."

"Well, until we find out exactly what's happening, we have to try our best to help these kids," Gaby said firmly.

"Maybe we can ask Ghostwriter to find more clues," Casey suggested.

"And check out the library," Lenni added. "We might be able to find out more about these clues there."

Suddenly Kevin Clarke rushed past the door of the meeting room. A gleam appeared in Alex's eye. "Miss the plane, Kevin?" he yelled.

Kevin stopped in his tracks, then turned around slowly. He walked back to the doorway of the room and stared at Alex.

"How come you're not at the Lakers game?" Alex asked him.

For a second, Kevin looked confused.

"Remember?" Jamal prodded him. "Yesterday you told us you and Malcolm couldn't come to the Halloween party because you had front-row tickets to the Lakers game."

"Uh . . ." Kevin's face turned red as he fumbled for words. "Yeah, well," he finally said, "Malcolm's gone. I—uh—can't find him anywhere."

"You mean he disappeared?" Gaby asked. "What are you talking about?"

"I was watching him after my mom went to work, and when I got out of the shower he was gone," Kevin explained. He looked around nervously. "I think he might have been abducted or something."

Alex kicked Gaby under the table. When she looked over at him, he mouthed the word *liar*.

Gaby turned back to Kevin, feeling a wave of anger wash over her. She'd had enough of Kevin

Clarke's stories. Yesterday he'd lied about his dad's getting tickets to the Lakers game, and today he had to save face by telling another lie—this time about Malcolm's being kidnapped.

"I can't believe Malcolm would just take off on his own," Kevin went on. "I know he was kidnapped."

"Yeah, right, Kevin," Gaby muttered as she turned away from Kevin and back to the casebook. "And my mother's a billionaire."

chapter seven

October 30, 1938

Sam tried not to panic as his cousin sat on the couch, gasping for breath. Her wheezing sounded more and more frantic. He had to do something, or else . . . Sam didn't want to think about the "or else."

Sam looked back at his journal. The ghost, or whatever the thing called Ghostwriter was, had said he would help, but now he was gone. And what about Sam's message to the team? It was still written on the page of the journal, so Ghostwriter hadn't taken it to them. Or had he?

Sam let out a sigh. Who were Ghostwriter and this team anyway? Did Alex, Gaby, Jamal, and the others live nearby? How could they possibly help him and Emily?

I'm waiting for a ghost and seven strangers to save

me and Emily, Sam thought. *This is crazy; we've got to do something ourselves.*

He glanced at his cousin. "Wait here, Emily," he said. "I'll try Mom again."

Sam wheeled his chair into the kitchen and reached for the phone. He tried to dial the pharmacy, and then the police, but the lines were still jammed.

Back in the living room, Emily stared at Sam with her huge blue eyes. Her face was a mask of terror as she wheezed and struggled to speak. "Did . . . you get . . . your mother?" she asked.

"No." Sam shook his head in frustration. He listened as another report came through on the radio. The broadcaster said the threat from the Martians was growing by the minute. An army of seven thousand men had tried to fight the creatures—only to be trampled to death or burned to cinders by their heat ray. Railroad tracks had been destroyed, and telephone communication across New Jersey and Pennsylvania was out.

"So much for the phone," Sam mumbled.

The strange thing was, everything sounded so quiet outside. How could a real war with Martians be happening out there?

"Sam," Emily choked out, "I . . . need help soon, or—"

"Don't even talk, Emily," Sam said. "It's okay. I'm going to get help. Don't worry—you'll see. It'll be okay. Everything's just fine."

Sam knew he was babbling, but he couldn't seem to stop himself. Desperately he glanced around the room. He had to do something. But with two broken legs he could barely get around, let alone help Emily.

Through the window, Sam could see headlights in the distance. *Maybe I can get out to the highway and flag somebody down,* he thought. It was a crazy idea, but so far it was the only one he had.

"I'll be back soon, Emily. Hang in there," he told his cousin. She nodded, then closed her eyes. Sam could see she was using all her strength to breathe.

Sam wheeled over to the front door. He leaned forward and stretched to grip the knob. Then he turned it and pushed the door with all his might.

It swung open.

I did it! Sam thought.

He rolled out onto the porch.

Then his heart sank. *How could I be such a dunce?* he thought. He'd forgotten about the steps that led down from the porch. There was no way he could make it down by himself in the chair.

"Dang it!" Sam exclaimed. He spun the chair around and rolled back into the living room.

Emily was watching his every move. "It's no use, Emily," he said. "I can't do anything in this stupid wheelchair." He looked down so she wouldn't see the tears springing into his eyes.

"Sam!" Emily gasped suddenly.

He looked up, watching her take a few shallow

breaths before she spoke again. "Take your time, Emily," he said softly.

"Look." Emily pointed to the sofa, where his journal was resting on one of the cushions. A light glowed weakly from the open pages. "It's . . . Ghostwriter," she managed to say.

Quickly Sam rolled himself over to the sofa and reached for the pen.

"Ghostwriter, I'm getting desperate! Emily's having an as~~X~~ta asthma attack, and I don't know what to do! If I don't get her some help, or some medicine, she might even die!"

Ghostwriter read Sam's words, then disappeared. A few seconds later, he returned and spelled out: Use to Tre Asth Only.

"What?" Sam mumbled out loud. This was no time for puzzles. What on earth was Ghostwriter saying?

"I don't understand, Ghostwriter," he penned quickly. "Can you tell me more?"

Ghostwriter came back in a flash with several more words. Iodine, Mercurochrome, Cotton Swabs, Zest Toothpaste.

Sam stared at the words in confusion. He'd asked Ghostwriter for help with Emily; why was he spelling out things that belonged in a pharmacy, or someone's medicine chest?

Medicine chest!

A second later, it hit him. A few months ago, when Emily had stayed over, Aunt Mary had sent

some asthma medicine with her. Maybe . . .

Sam rolled over to the bathroom. He struggled to maneuver the wheelchair into the tiny room and finally squeezed it through the doorway. Then he threw open the door of the medicine chest.

"Jeepers creepers," he whispered.

There, on the top shelf, next to the toothpaste and behind a bottle marked Iodine, was a small glass bottle. Most of the label had been rubbed away, but Sam could easily figure out what it used to say: Use to Treat Asthma Only.

The present, October 30

Alex reached for the pen again, then scribbled another note to Ghostwriter.

"We need more clues," he wrote. "Is there something else in Sam's house or journal that will help us find him and Emily?"

The team waited for Ghostwriter to come and read their message. Gaby tapped her foot nervously, trying to ignore the prickle of worry creeping up her spine. Why was Ghostwriter taking so long? Sam's note about the Martians had sounded desperate.

"He's back!" Casey's excited cry cut into Gaby's thoughts. "It's Ghostwriter!"

Gaby watched as Ghostwriter's glow swept dimly across the pages of her notebook. As she read the message from Sam, she gasped.

Ghostwriter, I'm getting desperate. Em-

ily's having an as̶h̶a asthma attack, and I don't know what to do! If I don't get her some help, or some medicine, she might even die!

"Oh my gosh," Lenni muttered. "Things are getting worse."

Ghostwriter read the note from Alex and the team about needing more clues, then disappeared.

A few minutes later, he was back. But this time, the message he brought with him glowed even more weakly. The words wobbled across the page.

"I can barely read this," Alex muttered.

Grovers Mill Trib
8–9 P.M. Mer
H. Wells
    Welles
Made with Pride in America by CRC

"Do you think these words are from Sam's journal?" Jamal asked.

"I'm not sure." Lenni frowned. "The first part may be from a newspaper. Maybe *Trib* is short for *Tribune.*"

Gaby quickly jotted that down. "That's a good idea, Lenni."

"Eight dash nine P.M. M-E-R" Tina said. "I wonder what that means."

"I have an idea." Hector jumped in. "Didn't

Sam say *Mercury Theatre* was his favorite show? Maybe that's when *Mercury Theatre* comes on TV."

"Could be," Jamal agreed. "What about CRC?"

" 'Made with Pride in America by CRC,' " Gaby read aloud. "Sounds like the name of a manufacturer."

The others nodded.

"What about the third clue?" said Gaby. "Why does it say Wells and then Welles, with an *e?*"

"It must be another of Sam's spelling mistakes," said Tina.

"This kid makes me look like a walking dictionary!" Hector said.

"Let's ask Ghostwriter if he can tell us more about where these clues are from," Gaby said. She grabbed her pen and wrote:

"Ghostwriter, can you tell us anything else about these clues? Are they from a newspaper or from Sam's journal?"

The team waited, but nothing happened.

"I have a feeling Ghostwriter's gone for a while," Alex said finally. "Let's do some research at the library, then try again."

"We'd better find Tamara first," Tina said, "and make sure she doesn't need any more help before tonight."

Gaby agreed. "Kevin already let her down," she said. "I don't want do the same thing."

On the way out, the team found Tamara setting

up a table for the refreshments. Jamal told her they needed to go to the library, if it was okay with her.

"I'm fine for now," Tamara replied. "Just make sure you're back here by six tonight in your costumes. The party starts at seven-thirty."

The team promised they'd be there in full costume.

"You guys are doing homework on a weekend?" Tamara asked.

"Not exactly," Tina told her. "We need to find out where Grovers Mill, New Jersey, is."

"Grovers Mill?" Tamara thought for a minute. "For some reason, it sounds familiar, but I can't place it," she said finally. "Good luck, guys. I'll see you tonight."

They said good-bye and left the center.

As Gaby hurried down the steps behind the others, she thought about how desperate Sam's last message had sounded. Gaby didn't know much about asthma except that it was a very serious disease.

Sam must know it, too, Gaby thought, remembering what he'd written about Emily.

If I don't get her some help, or some medicine, she might even die. . . .

chapter eight

October 30, 1938

"Thank you, Ghostwriter!" Sam murmured as his eyes fixed on the brown medicine bottle in his family's medicine chest. "You're a lifesaver." If it hadn't been for Ghostwriter, Sam never would have thought of the medication for Emily.

Now all he had to do was find a way to reach it from his wheelchair.

Sam backed the wheelchair out of the bathroom and rolled into the living room. Emily stared at him, tears streaming down her face. "The . . . Martians, Sam." She gulped air. "They're all over!"

Sam froze and listened to the radio announcer describing the view from the roof of the broadcasting building in New York City. It sounded like total panic. Bridges and roads leading to and from the city were jammed. People everywhere were screaming and running for their lives.

"Wait a minute!" the announcer cried. "A bulletin's been handed to me. Martian cylinders are falling all over the country. People are running toward the East River. . . . thousands of them dropping in like rats . . ."

"*NO!*" Sam screamed, and put his hands over his ears. A second later he rolled over to the radio in his chair and snapped it off. "I can't listen any longer," he declared.

"Oh . . . Sam," Emily sobbed. Her whole body trembled violently, and she was still wheezing and gasping for air.

"It's all right, Emily," Sam said desperately. "Everything's going to be okay."

Frantically he looked around the room. He couldn't stop the Martians, but maybe he could find a way to get the medicine for Emily.

Finally he noticed a wooden hanger lying on the floor near a closet. He wheeled the chair over, scooped it up, then started for the bathroom again.

Sweat was dripping down his face as he inched his chair into the narrow room. Holding out the hanger, he reached toward the brown vial in the medicine chest.

"Easy, Sam," he told himself. "Stay steady."

Carefully he looped the hanger over the bottle. Then he yanked on the hanger, and the bottle began to fall. With his other hand, Sam reached

up to catch it. For a second his fingers grazed the

medicine bottle. Then the bottle slipped past his outstretched fingers and toppled to the floor.

Sam stared in horror as the bottle of asthma medicine—his only hope—shattered in a hundred pieces.

The present, October 30

"I found it!" Alex exclaimed as he and the rest of the team huddled around the map of New Jersey that was spread open on the table at the Fort Greene Public Library. "Grovers Mill, right here," he said, pointing to the spot.

"It looks like it's about an hour away from Fort Greene," Jamal said. "I just can't figure this out." He shook his head. "If aliens have really landed this close to where we live, how come we haven't heard a word about it?"

"It's very bizarre," Lenni agreed.

"Hey, guys," Hector called out softly. "Ghost-writer's back. And I think he's got more of Sam's journal."

The team glanced down at an open book lying beside Casey.

Gaby's mouth dropped open as she read the words Sam had recorded.

The Martains' faces look like leather and saliva drips off their lips, which quiver and pulsate.

"They sound so real," Casey whispered.

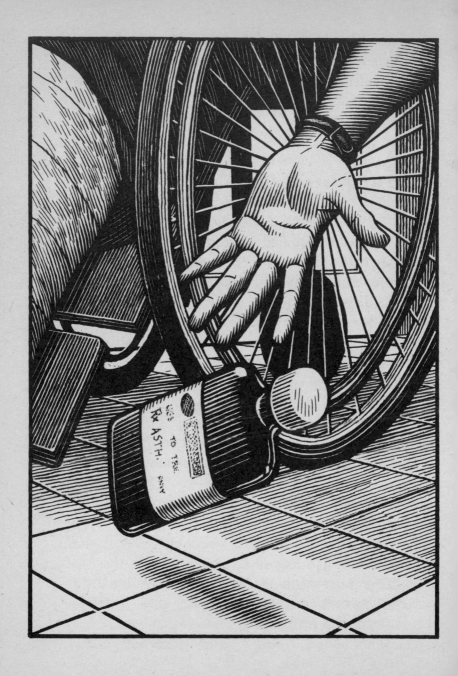

Alex bit his lip. "I still say we're missing something. Hey, Hector, ask Ghostwriter—"

"Too late," Hector interrupted. "He just faded."

"He seems really tired today, doesn't he?" Tina put in.

Gaby nodded as she glanced over at the reference desk. "Maybe I'll ask the librarian if he knows anything about Martians in New Jersey," she said, then hurried over to where the young man sat typing at a computer keyboard.

"Excuse me, sir." Gaby hesitated for a second, then blurted out, "Have you heard anything about aliens landing in New Jersey today?"

Slowly the librarian glanced up at Gaby. As he stared at her and adjusted his glasses, a grin crept across his face. "Not exactly," he replied finally. "But I did read that the president is speaking in Hackensack."

"I'm not kidding around," Gaby began to protest, but by now the librarian's grin had turned into loud laughter.

"I think you and your friends are reading too many comic books," he said.

"Never mind," Gaby mumbled, her face turning red. "Thanks anyway."

When Gaby returned to the table, Casey was showing the team one of her books on UFOs and arguing that it was possible that Martians *had* invaded Sam's town.

"You can call it nonsense, Alex," she said. "But

people have reported seeing UFOs for the last ten thousand years. The Greeks and Romans saw weird lights in the sky, and so did people living in the Middle Ages."

Hector was reading over her shoulder. "Hmmm. This section says that people most frequently report being *abducted* by UFOs in the United States. Maybe Kevin Clarke *is* telling the truth."

"This doesn't help us figure out what's going on with Sam and Emily," Lenni said impatiently. "And I'm worried about Emily. Asthma is very serious. She could be in real trouble."

Gaby had been thinking the same thing ever since they'd left the center. "The librarian didn't know anything about aliens in New Jersey," she said grimly.

"Let's get cracking," Jamal said. "We can split up the clues we have so far and do some research."

Gaby pulled the casebook out of her backpack. First the team reread the clues from Sam's journal:

CLUES

1. Sam and Emily are cousins who live in Grovers Mill, New Jersey.

2. They like two TV shows, Mercury Theatre and Bergen & McCarthy.

3. Sam has two broken legs.

4. There's a situation in Czechoslovakia and Europe. Bad guy (?) with the initials A̶M̶. A.H. is causing trouble.

Then they reread the other clues that Ghostwriter had brought. They still weren't sure where these had come from—Sam's journal or somewhere else inside his house.

Grovers Mill Trib
8–9 P.M. Mer
H. Wells
  Welles
Made with Pride in America by CRC

"Why don't Lenni and Gaby look up H. Wells?" Alex suggested. "And Jamal and I can try to track down a copy of the *Grovers Mill Tribune*."

"Hector, Tina, and I can try to get more information about the 'situation in Czechoslovakia and Europe,'" Casey put in. "Maybe we can figure out who A.H. is."

Alex pointed to Sam's crossout right before the initials *A.H.* "It looks like the guy's first name begins with *A-d,*" he said.

"How do we know it's a bad guy, not a bad *woman?*" Tina said.

"Good point," Alex said. "Check both out, guys."

Lenni stared at the remaining clues. "What about 'Made with Pride in America by CRC'?" she asked.

"We'll look up that, too," Gaby said. "It sounds like a company. We should be able to find something. Come on, let's get going."

Forty-five minutes later, the team met again at the table near the maps.

"I think we were wrong about the *Tribune,*" Jamal reported. "Alex and I looked it up. There used to be a paper called the *Tribune,* but they stopped printing it about thirty years ago."

"We also looked at a bunch of TV listings," Alex put in. "We couldn't find any TV shows called *Bergen & McCarthy* or *Mercury Theatre.*"

Lenni pointed to a pile of books on the table. "Gaby and I think that H. Wells might be H. G. Wells, a famous science fiction writer," she said. "He wrote a ton of novels and essays; I'm going to check some of them out."

Casey sighed. "We couldn't find out much at all. We looked at copies of *The New York Times* from the last month. There wasn't anything about a situation in Czechoslovakia or a war in Europe."

"And the only A.H. we could find in the head-lines is a guy named Adam Halley," Hector added. "He's a peace activist from Berkeley, California. I don't think he's the one Sam was talking about who's been making trouble."

"It's as if Sam's from another world," Gaby said. "I mean, nothing matches."

"What about *CRC?*" Jamal asked. "Did you find that?"

Gaby shrugged. "It probably stands for Continental Radio Company. They've been around for a long time. The company makes electronics—radios, stereos, stuff like that."

"That must be who made Sam's TV," Hector said.

Gaby nodded, then said, "But so what? That still doesn't tell us anything."

Lenni stood up and fished in her backpack for her library card. "Maybe one of these books will tell us something," she said. "I have four novels by H. G. Wells: *The Time Machine, The Invisible Man, The War of the Worlds,* and *Ann Veronica,* and some books of essays, too."

"Did you look up the other Welles?" asked Jamal. "The name with the *e* in it?"

Gaby shook her head. "No. I thought we decided Sam had just made another spelling mistake," she said.

"Oh, right." Jamal tapped himself on the head. "I forgot."

Suddenly the lights inside the library began to flicker.

"Uh-oh." Lenni scooped up the books by H. G. Wells. "The library closes in fifteen minutes. I'd better get these checked out."

The library was closing and they hadn't learned anything at all about Grovers Mill and what was happening there, Gaby thought, feeling frustrated. Plus she still couldn't shake the thought of Emily from her head.

A few minutes later Lenni came back with the books by H. G. Wells. "We'd better go," Gaby said reluctantly.

As they headed back into the cold air, Gaby felt as if she were abandoning Sam and Emily. But she didn't know what else to do. The library was closing down for the day, and in just a few hours the community center would be opening its doors for the Haunted Halloween Party.

chapter nine

"**I**'ve come to suck your blood!"

Gaby shrieked as Alex suddenly grabbed her from behind.

He let out an evil-sounding laugh. "Do not *vorry*, my dear. Vee wampires do not take blood from *vitches* like you."

Gaby shook free of her brother and turned around to look at him in his vampire costume. He had on black pants, a white shirt, and a long, flowing black cape. Neon-green fangs glowed from inside his mouth, and white makeup covered his cheeks and forehead.

"I hate to admit it, Alex, but for once you look great!" Gaby told him. "You make a fabulous vampire."

"You look pretty scary yourself," Alex said.

"Thanks." Gaby checked her reflection again in

the mirror. She was also dressed all in black, with green makeup smeared over her face. On her head was a pointy witch's hat, and skeleton earrings dangled from her ears.

"I'm almost ready," she told Alex. "I just want to black out a few of my teeth. I bought this really cool makeup."

"Hurry up," Alex replied. "We've got to leave in about five minutes."

Gaby nodded and leaned closer to the mirror to see her teeth better. As she began to color them with the makeup, a tiny strip of paper on her dresser caught her eye.

Things are not what they seem.

It was her fortune from the other night. For a second, Gaby thought back to the Chinese dinner at Lenni's apartment. Just a few days ago, the team members had been teasing Gaby and Casey for even wondering if UFOs were real. Now here they all were, investigating a case involving Martians that had landed in New Jersey!

Gaby shook her head. This was definitely one of the strangest cases the team had ever tried to solve.

"Come on, Gaby." Alex pounded on the door of her room, startling her.

Impulsively she scooped up the fortune on her dresser and stuck it in the pocket of her witch's costume. Then she quickly finished turning herself into an ugly old hag.

* * *

"**H**ey, look who's back from outer space!" Alex called out as he and Gaby walked up the steps of the Fort Greene Community Center thirty minutes later.

Gaby looked up. A small boy dressed in a pirate costume and carrying a plastic jack-o'-lantern ducked into the center ahead of them. It was Malcolm Clarke, Kevin's younger brother.

"I wonder if the aliens who abducted Malcolm took him trick-or-treating on Jupiter," Gaby said, grinning.

She and Alex laughed as they entered the community center.

Then they both stopped in their tracks.

The community center had been totally transformed. Over the doorway, tiny jack-o'-lantern lights blinked on and off. Black plastic spiders dangled from a lacy web on the ceiling. Fake tombstones painted in Day-Glo colors were scattered around the room.

"It looks awesome in here," Alex said. "Check out the tunes, too." Eerie music blasted from the speakers of Tamara's portable stereo.

Gaby laughed as Alex began twirling his cape and dancing to the howls and screeches coming from the stereo. "Nice moves, Count Dracula," she said. "I wonder where Tamara found this creepy tape."

As Gaby crouched next to the stereo to check out the cassette inside, something caught her eye. Running along the top of the radio and tape player was a narrow silver band stamped with the words *Made with Pride in America by CRC.*

Gaby frowned. "Hey, Alex," she called. "Come over here for a second."

● Attention, Reader: Can you guess what Gaby has figured out?
—Ghostwriter

Gaby was about to call her brother again when Kevin Clarke burst into the room.

"Oh." He drew back, looking surprised to see Gaby and Alex.

Alex stopped dancing and bared his fangs. *"Vell,* look who it is. Don't tell me you changed your mind and decided to drop in for the party."

"Not exactly, Dracula," Kevin retorted. "I don't care about the stupid Haunted Halloween Party. I've spent the whole day looking for Malcolm. I know he's been kidnapped."

Gaby folded her arms and stared at Kevin. *How can he keep telling lies?* she wondered. Alex and Gaby had seen the little boy going into the center ten minutes before.

"Oh, cut it out, Kevin," Gaby snapped impatiently as Kevin began describing how Malcolm had been wearing his pirate costume before he'd disappeared that morning. "No one believes a word you say anymore."

Kevin stopped in midsentence and narrowed his eyes at Gaby. For a second, Gaby thought he was going to say something back, but then he seemed to change his mind. Abruptly he wheeled around and stalked over to the pay phone.

Just then the rest of the team entered the center.

"Hey, Gaby!" Casey yelled.

Gaby laughed as Casey approached. She was dressed in a brightly colored clown's outfit, with a big red nose and a funny-looking hat perched on her head.

"Cool costume!" Alex told her.

"Isn't this hat great?" Casey took off the hat and held it out for him to inspect more closely.

"Yeah, it's—" Alex yelped as the flower poking up from the hat squirted water right in his face.

The others laughed.

"Sorry about that, Alex." Casey grinned. "I couldn't resist."

"No problem, Casey," he mumbled. "I just hope it didn't ruin my makeup."

"You look great," Gaby told Casey. She turned to the rest of the team. "So do you guys."

Jamal had on his monster costume, and Hector was dressed as a glow-in-the-dark skeleton.

Alex looked at Lenni's black-and-white-striped costume and laughed. "Are you supposed to be a zebra?" he asked.

She held up a plastic black ball dangling from a chain. "Nope—a convict."

"Everyone will know what I am," Tina said.

Gaby took one look at the pointy ears on Tina's head and the whiskers painted on her face, then nodded. "A black cat."

Jamal jerked a thumb at Kevin, who was still talking on the pay phone. "What was up with him?"

"Oh, the usual pack of lies," Gaby replied.

"More UFO stuff," Alex added. "You have to admit, he doesn't give up. That guy is unbelievable."

"Never mind him." Lenni changed the subject. "Has anybody heard from Ghostwriter?"

The team members shook their heads.

"I'm worried about him—and Sam and Emily, too," Tina said.

"What about those books by H. G. Wells, Lenni?" Hector asked. "Did you find anything interesting?"

"I was so busy getting my costume ready for the party, I only had time to flip through them," Lenni admitted. "I brought them with me, just in case I get a minute." She paused, then said, "At first I thought one of the books, *The War of the Worlds,* might turn up something."

"Why?" asked Jamal.

"It's a novel about Martians invading the world."

"A Martian invasion?" Alex echoed. "That sounds familiar!"

Lenni shook her head. "I think it's just a weird coincidence. The book takes place in England, not the United States, and it seemed pretty different from what Sam described."

Suddenly Gaby remembered what she'd been about to tell Alex before Kevin Clarke had showed up. She pointed to Tamara's portable stereo. "See that metal strip?" she asked.

" 'Made with Pride in America by CRC,' " Alex read aloud.

"Hey," Casey said. "That's one of the clues Ghostwriter brought us!"

"You said they make electronic stuff, right? Stereos, radios, TVs . . . ," Alex said.

Gaby shook her head. "We just assumed they made TVs," she corrected him. "All it said in the book at the library was that the company made stereos and radios."

Lenni studied her face. "What are you saying, Gaby?"

Jamal ripped the monster mask off his face before Gaby could answer. "She's saying that Sam and Emily are listening to the radio—not watching TV!" he guessed.

"Exactly!" Gaby confirmed.

"That would explain why we couldn't find *Mercury Theatre* or *Bergen & McCarthy* in the TV listings," Tina added.

Casey looked doubtful. "But who listens to shows on the radio?" she asked. "I mean, my aunt and uncle do, but they're grown-ups. Kids mostly listen to music on the radio."

"What difference does it make?" Alex put in. "So Sam and Emily are listening to the radio, not watching TV. It doesn't help us figure out what's going on."

"Maybe—" Hector began.

"There you are!" Tamara Battle strode into the room, coming from one of the storage areas in the back. She had on a huge soda-can costume made out of cardboard and felt.

"Hey, look at you!" Alex grinned. "I was just getting thirsty!"

Tamara laughed. "My husband whipped this up for me. Isn't it great? Wait till you see Hank's costume," she added. "He's supposed to be an ax murderer!"

"Cool!" Hector said.

Tamara pulled out her clipboard and began calling out instructions. "Gaby, you'll be in the little room off to the right with your cauldron. I've already filled it with dry ice, so it'll smoke and look really cool. Hector and Lenni, please put the spaghetti and grapes out in the bowls. Jamal and Casey, can you please help me finish up the goody bags?"

The team scattered all over the center, making last-minute preparations for the party. Gaby took her place near the cauldron. Inside, the dry-ice was sending up white smoke. *It does look pretty cool,* Gaby thought. *The kids will love it.*

As she began to practice stirring the fake potion, she found herself wishing that she really did have magic powers. The first thing she'd do would be to cast a spell to help find Sam and Emily.

chapter ten

October 30, 1938

Sam stared at the pieces of glass scattered around the room and under the wheels of his chair. He could feel his fingers beginning to tremble.

"Oh my gosh," he whispered. "What am I going to do now?" Emily's asthma medicine was in a puddle on the floor.

Sam reached for the pen lying on his lap. Maybe the ghost had another idea.

"Ghostwriter?" he wrote. "Are you there?"

Sam waited a few minutes, but there was no reply. With a heavy heart, he decided he'd better go check on Emily.

Don't panic, Sam, he told himself. *Ghostwriter is trying to help you. The team is bound to arrive soon. Unless the Martians beat them to the front door.*

The present, October 30

In a back room at the community center, Jamal and Casey helped Tamara stick a few more plastic spiders and stickers into the kids' goody bags and then tie up the "hands" with orange and black ribbon.

As they worked, Casey told Jamal that more than thirty sightings of UFOs had been reported in Brooklyn during the past year.

"Plus, in the book I'm reading," she went on, "one lady said aliens kidnapped her from her campsite in Maine, then took her fishing."

"Fishing?" Jamal rolled his eyes at his cousin, then said, "That's a new one!"

"And there's this old man from Puerto Rico who . . ." Casey spent the next few minutes telling him more "true" stories about people who'd been abducted.

"You know, Casey," Jamal began. "It's cool you're interested in UFOs and all, but . . ."

Casey looked at him. "But what?" she asked. Then she let out a sigh. "Never mind. I know what you're going to say. Exactly what Alex and Grandma CeCe and Gaby and everyone else has been saying—that I'm gullible and stupid for believing in UFOs."

Suddenly she stood up and pushed the pile of hands she'd been working on into the center of the table. "I'll see you later, Jamal," she mumbled. "I've got other stuff to do."

"Casey, wait . . ." Jamal started to say something more, then decided to just let her go. "Oh well," he mumbled to Tamara, who'd been listening to the whole thing from the other end of the table. He hadn't meant to hurt Casey's feelings, but he did want to tell her he thought she was getting carried away. He'd have to try to talk to her again, maybe after the party.

A few minutes later Jamal finished tying up the last hand in his pile. "I'm done," he announced.

"I've got two more," Tamara told him. "Then we can bring these out front for Casey to give out later."

As Tamara kept working, Jamal pulled out the casebook and began studying the clues again. *The team has to be missing a piece of the puzzle,* he thought. The situation was just too weird. How could Martians be invading a town like Grovers Mill, New Jersey, without the rest of the world's knowing?

He read over Sam's journal entry, thinking about Gaby's radio theory. What if she was right? Would that make a difference in how they read the clues?

He stopped when he came to the part about the news interruptions.

"*. . . Lately there have been a lot of news updates. According to the newspapers and the presadent, the situation in Czechoslovakia (I looked up the spelling of this one in my geog-*

raphy book!) and the rest of Europe is getting worse . . ."

What is Sam talking about? Jamal wondered. He had been watching TV and listening to the radio on and off for the past week. As far as he could recall, there hadn't been any special reports about a situation in Europe or Czechoslovakia.

Puzzled, he took out his pen and circled that part of the journal. As Gaby had said earlier, Sam lived close to them, yet it was as if he were in a different world.

"Finished!" Tamara exclaimed from across the table. She stood to gather up the goody bags and toss them in a big basket. "History test on Monday?" she asked, suddenly noticing the open notebook in front of Jamal. "Judging by the fact that you're studying on a weekend, I bet you'll get an A."

"Huh?" Jamal looked up. He'd been so lost in his thoughts, he hadn't heard a word she'd said.

"Big test on Monday?" Tamara repeated. She pointed to the word *Czechoslovakia,* which was circled in the notebook. "Didn't that country break up into two countries a few years ago?" she asked. "I think one's called the Czech Republic and the other one is . . . Oh, never mind." She quickly scooped up the basket of goody bags and glanced at her watch. "It's almost time," she said. "See you in a few minutes."

Jamal stared at Tamara as she hurried away.

The Czech Republic? Her words were echoing inside his head. One of the new names for Czechoslovakia was the Czech Republic?

Suddenly it clicked. The missing piece of the puzzle snapped into place.

Jamal jumped to his feet. If he hurried, he'd have just enough time before the Halloween party began to tell the team what he'd figured out.

October 30, 1938

When Sam rolled his wheelchair back into the living room, Emily was lying on the couch, her eyes closed. Her face looked deathly white.

"Emily!" Sam cried, his heart racing.

A second later, his cousin's eyes fluttered open. Relief washed over Sam. Emily was okay. She opened her mouth to speak, wheezing from the effort.

"Oh my gosh," Sam said. "I thought . . ." His words trailed off as he saw how scared and desperate she looked. "Never mind, Em," he whispered. "Don't try to talk. Help is coming. I know it is. I haven't heard from Ghostwriter yet, but he'll be back soon."

Sam tried to reassure Emily as best he could. He wasn't sure how much time had passed since Ghostwriter had promised to return with help, but it felt like forever. *Mom would tell me this is total foolishness,* he thought. *Depending on a ghost to save me and Emily!*

If only there was something else he could do on his own.

Sam glanced out the window. A flash of light suddenly caught his eye. Strange-looking yellow beams were shooting across the sky over Sam's house.

What's happening now? Sam wondered. For a moment, he was tempted to turn the radio back on. Then he thought better of it. More bad news would only make Emily's asthma worse.

Instead, Sam began writing another note to the team in his journal. He kept pausing to look up at the odd yellow lights probing the night sky.

Ice-cold terror settled deep in his bones.

The present, October 30

Jamal quickly found Alex and Tina, who were dumping the peeled grapes into a large basin. "Help me round up the rest of the team," he said. "We need to rally before the party starts." As the three of them scattered, Jamal tried to ignore the fact that the minutes were ticking by. How much time did they have to help Sam and Emily? he wondered. He didn't want to think about what would happen to Emily if they were too late.

Five minutes later, the team had gathered near the entrance to the community center.

"What's up, Jamal?" Lenni asked.

"I think I've figured out one of the clues from Sam's journal," he told them. "Remember how Sam said there was a situation in Europe and Czechoslovakia?"

Tina nodded. "But we couldn't find anything in the news about that. Or who that guy A.H. is."

"Right," Jamal went on. "A few minutes ago Tamara saw the word *Czechoslovakia* circled in the casebook, and she told me that that was the *old* name for that country."

"The old name?" Lenni repeated. "What do you mean?"

"She said that the name of the country had changed a few years ago," Jamal said. "And then I started thinking about how Ghostwriter keeps fading and disappearing for long stretches."

Gaby slapped a hand over her mouth. "Oh my gosh," she said. "I can't believe we didn't figure this out earlier!"

Casey was still confused. "What are you guys talking about?"

Jamal turned to her. "Think about it, Casey. When was the last time that Ghostwriter disappeared for a while and started to lose his powers?"

She wrinkled her nose. "When he traveled back in time," she began. "When he— Oh, I get it!"

"So Sam and Emily are from the past, too!"

Hector said. "Ghostwriter's traveling through time again!"

"That's right!" Tina exclaimed. "The last time Ghostwriter kept fading like he's been doing today, he was trying to help Frank Flynn, that boy who used to live in Jamal's house in 1928."

"Exactly." Jamal held out the casebook, and the team looked over the clues. "I bet we can figure out a way to help Sam and Emily, if we can figure out what time period they're from."

"Well, we know they listened to the radio," Tina said, "so they have to be living after the radio was invented."

"And before the 1990s," Jamal said. "That was when Czechoslovakia was renamed."

Hector traced Sam's journal entry with his finger, trying to find a particular line. " 'When she drove away . . . ,' " Hector read aloud. "Sam's mother has a car—it couldn't have been *too* long ago."

"He's probably from the twentieth century. Most people had cars by the 1920s or 1930s, I think," Alex said.

Lenni thought about Alex's remark. Then her eye went back to two of the letters that Sam had crossed out—*Ad*. The initials A.H. followed his crossout. "So who is this guy?" she wondered out loud. "And what was happening in Europe during the 1920s and 1930s?"

"World War One?" Gaby said.

Lenni shook her head. "I think that war started before 1920," she said. "But maybe Sam's talking about World War Two."

Casey looked worried. "How are we going to figure this out?" she asked. "Poor Emily. If we don't help her . . ."

Tina jumped to her feet. "I bet Hank Delaney can tell us," she said. "I'll be right back."

When she returned a few minutes later, there was a broad grin on her face. "You were right, Lenni," Tina began. "Hank told me that World War One was over by 1918, and World War Two began in 1939. So A.H. is—"

"Adolf Hitler!" Alex exclaimed before Tina could finish. "When Hitler tried to take over parts of Europe, World War Two broke out. I bet that's what Sam meant by the 'situation in Europe.'"

Gaby beamed. "Now we're getting somewhere," she said. "But we'd better make sure we're on the right track. Let's see if Ghostwriter is strong enough to get another note to Sam."

Gaby took the notebook back from Jamal and started to draft a message. Then she noticed a weak glow.

It was Ghostwriter.

"He's got a message from Sam," Jamal said as he struggled to read the faint words on the page.

"Don't fade on us, Ghostwriter, buddy," Alex murmured.

Finally the message came in clearly enough for the team to read.

Dear Team,

Emily's asthma is getting worse and I don't know what to do. Outside I can see strange-looking lights in the sky. The news from the radio was so ter- ribel, I turned it off. The Martains have destroyed Newark and New York City. I think this might be the end of the world. I don't know what's hap- pened to my mother or the rest of my family and friends. We're trapped here. Please help—as soon as you can.

—Sam

Gaby stared at her friends. "Newark *and* New York City, destroyed by Martians?" she said. "This can't be possible."

"That never happened for real, did it?" Casey asked. "I mean, I've been reading lots about UFOs, and I haven't come across a single word about New York City or Newark being destroyed."

Jamal shook his head. "I don't know what's go- ing on. But now I'm more convinced than ever that Sam is from the past."

Lenni nodded. "We've got to find out the date, though. Quick, Gaby, write back and find out what year he's from."

Gaby nodded, then finished her note to Sam. She knew she'd better keep it short—from the look of things, Ghostwriter might not have enough strength to carry a long message back through time.

DEAR SAM,
WE'RE TRYING TO FIND A WAY TO HELP
YOU. WE KNOW IT'S OCTOBER 30 — CAN
YOU TELL US WHAT YEAR?

The team watched as Ghostwriter slowly swept across the page.

"Now we have to wait for an answer," Lenni said grimly.

"Maybe I'll try to call my grandmother in the meantime," Jamal said. "She can probably tell me something about the old radio shows that Sam and Emily like."

"Okay, everybody." Tamara's voice suddenly rang out through the center.

"Uh-oh, the party's about to start," Casey said. "They need us."

Tamara strode toward the main doors of the center. "It's showtime, everybody," she called. Jamal and Alex hurried after her.

Alex adjusted his cape, then reached for the doors. A second later, he flung them open.

Outside, on the steps, Gaby could see candles flickering inside paper-bag lanterns. A big crowd of kids in costumes stood there, eager for the fun to begin.

Alex waved his cape with a flourish, then put on a creepy vampire voice. *"Velcome* to the Haunted Halloween Party," he said.

A few of the youngest kids screamed and backed away in fright.

"Hi, Dracula!" a little boy dressed as a dalmatian cried.

Then, one by one, the kids climbed up the steps and lined up to follow Alex on the spooky tour around the center.

Gaby put her witch's hat back on her head and took her position beside the smoking cauldron.

As the parade of ghosts and goblins snaked past her, she could feel a knot forming inside her stomach.

Halloween is supposed to be scary, she thought. But what was happening to Sam and Emily was more frightening than any Halloween fright Gaby had ever encountered.

chapter eleven

"Eyes of newt, witch hazel root," Gaby chanted as she stirred the cauldron of dry ice. She didn't know where Tamara had gotten the dry ice, but it was smoking like crazy. As the little kids walked by, they stared at her, amazed by the sight of "Witch Gabriela" and her bubbling cauldron.

If it hadn't been for the fact that she was worrying about Sam and Emily, she would have been having a great time at the Haunted Halloween Party. So far none of the team members had heard from Ghostwriter. Gaby couldn't help wondering if her note about the date had ever reached Sam.

"*Aaaaaa!*"

Suddenly another loud shriek came from next door, where Lenni and Hector were letting kids touch the "monster eyeballs," "human guts," and "witch's scalp."

A few minutes later, Tamara stuck her head in the door. "We're getting ready to serve some snacks, Gaby. Can you help pass out the witch's brew you made?"

"Sure," Gaby replied.

"What's in it, anyway?" Tamara asked.

"Oh, just some roaches, snakes, and rat skulls," Gaby said. "Stuff like that."

Tamara grimaced. "Sounds delicious."

Gaby followed Tamara to the main room of the center, where several long tables had been set up. The kids were beginning to sit down for the snacks. Gaby smiled at all the costumes—she saw a ballerina, a mouse, several superheroes, a dinosaur, two football players, and a kid who had dressed as a computer.

As Gaby helped serve her concoction of roaches (raisins), dragon's eyes (peppermints), and rat skulls (marshmallows), she noticed Kevin Clarke standing a few feet away. He was speaking softly into the receiver of the pay phone again.

As Gaby went over to give the little dinosaur and two knights their brew, she could hear a few words Kevin was saying.

". . . I know you took him. You'd better bring him back right away. . . . It's called kidnapping, you know. . . ."

"Gimme a break," Gaby muttered. "Is he pretending to call outer space now?" She finished serving the brew, then joined Lenni and Casey at the opposite end of the room. "Kevin's still at it," she told them, and repeated what she'd heard him saying.

"What if Malcolm really did get kidnapped?" Casey said.

"Come on, Casey," Lenni said. "We've been trying to tell you—the guy's a liar with a capital *L*."

"I feel sorry for him." Casey shrugged.

Just then Jamal and Alex hurried over.

"Hey, you guys," Jamal called out. "Guess what? I just talked to my grandmother. She knows a lot about old radio shows. She told me that *Bergen & McCarthy* used to be really popular."

"What about *Mercury Theatre?*" Lenni asked. "Did she know anything about that show?"

"She wasn't positive, but she thought it might have been the name of an old radio show a man named Orson Welles did. It was on at the same time as *Bergen & McCarthy.*"

By this time Hector and Tina had joined the rest of the team.

Gaby stared at Jamal. "Did you say 'Welles,' Jamal?"

Jamal nodded. "That's right. Orson Welles. My grandmother said she was too young to remember his show very well, but she thinks her parents used to listen to it."

"I'll be right back," Gaby said suddenly. She hurried over to the storage room where she'd left her coat and her backpack containing the casebook. She grabbed the notebook and went back to her friends.

"Look at this!" she said, pointing to one of the clues Ghostwriter had brought them earlier that day.

"Oh my gosh," Casey whispered.

Grovers Mill Trib
8–9 P.M. Mer
H. Wells
    Welles
Made with Pride in America by CRC

● Attention, Reader: Can you figure out what Gaby has thought of? Which clue is she pointing to?

                    —Ghostwriter

The team stared at their casebook. Gaby's finger was on the word *Welles.*

"I wonder how you spell Orson's last name," Tina said. "Could there be an *e* at the end?"

"That's exactly what I'm wondering, Tina," Gaby said.

"I think there's an old encyclopedia in the office in the back room," Jamal said. "Maybe I can look it up."

"I'll do it," Alex said, racing for the back room.

"So what if there are two different Wellses?" Lenni asked. "What's the connection?"

"That's what we have to figure out," Gaby told her.

A few minutes later, Alex hurried toward them, waving a thick, tattered paperback. "Wait till you guys hear this!"

October 30, 1938

Sam sat frozen in his wheelchair as the pulsing yellow lights lit up his window. They seemed to grow more intense by the minute. Now they were traveling up and down, as if they were scanning Sam's house.

Sam glanced over at Emily, who was sitting up on the couch, her eyes wide with terror.

Then Sam noticed his journal. The letters were swirling again!

But this time the letters were very faint. What was the team—or Ghostwriter—trying to say?

Finally Sam managed to make out the words.

Dear Sam,
    We're trying to find a way to help you. We know it's October 30—can you tell us what year?

The year? Sam thought. *Why is the team asking me about the year at a time like this? Don't they already know the year?*

His spirits sinking, Sam wrote back: "October 30, 1938." He didn't see how this could possibly help him and Emily.

Sam watched Ghostwriter wobbling across the page as if he was struggling to read what Sam had written.

The ghost seems so tired, Sam thought. *I wonder . . .*

A sudden sound made Sam look up from the journal.

Crunch. Crunch. Crunch.

Someone was approaching along the pebble-lined path outside.

It's the Martians! Sam thought.

Crunch. Crunch. Crunch.

The sound drew closer and closer.

And then came the yellow light, boring right through the window, blinding Sam with its bright beam.

Sam sank back into his wheelchair, holding up his hands to shield his eyes and face.

It's over, he thought. *It's too late to save Emily and too late to save me. The Martians are right outside my door, about to come in!*

The present, October 30

"Listen to this," Alex said to his friends. He opened the book to the section where the Ws were listed and read aloud the entry under Welles.

" 'While the American actor and director Orson Welles worked in theater and movies for almost fifty years, he is best known for a project he finished before he turned thirty. The project was his 1938 radio adaptation of a novel by H. G. Wells, The War of the Worlds, for the Mercury Theatre of the Air. In adapting the story for radio, the producers used the device of a news broadcast, which made many people believe that Martians had actually invaded the U.S. . . .' "

Jamal shot up out of his seat as if he'd gotten an electric shock. "It's a hoax!" he cried. "The Martian invasion is a radio show, not a news broadcast!"

"You mean what Sam and Emily are listening to is the novel I brought home from the library?" Lenni asked.

"That's got to be it," Jamal replied. "The producers must have changed the book for the radio show."

"We've got to let Sam and Emily know!" Hector exclaimed. "They think the world's about to end!"

"But how?" Gaby wailed. "We haven't even heard from Ghostwriter about the date. How do we know he's got enough power left to carry another message?"

"We've got to try, Gaby," Alex broke in. He grabbed his pen and scrawled a message to Sam and Emily.

"Keep it short, Alex," Tina reminded him. "We don't want Ghostwriter to have to work too hard."

SAM AND EMILY,
IT'S A HOAX! THE MARTIANS AREN'T REAL.
YOU'RE LISTENING TO A STORY BY H. G.
WELLS, NOT A NEWS BROADCAST.

The team stared at the page, waiting for Ghostwriter to come and carry away their words.

Gaby was so nervous, she could barely stand still. She stood up and paced around the room, watching the little kids gobbling up their spider cookies and witch's brew.

Then Tamara clapped her hands. "It's time for ghost stories, guys. Everybody make a circle."

None of the team members spoke as they kept staring at the page where Alex had written the message.

Nothing happened. Ghostwriter was gone.

chapter twelve

Gaby's spirits were sinking as she helped Tamara arrange the kids in a circle on the floor. Where was Ghostwriter? Were his powers gone for good? Without Ghostwriter, the team had absolutely no way to help Sam and Emily.

It's over, Gaby realized. *We blew it. If only the team had been able to solve the mystery more quickly, then maybe Emily's asthma . . .* She couldn't even bear to think about it.

Hank Delaney dimmed the lights. Then he sat in front of the children, a single candle lit in front of him. With a dark, jagged scar and streaks of blood painted on his face, along with the ax laid in front of him, Hank definitely looked the part of a real ax murderer.

Gaby stood at the edge of the circle, listening as he began telling a ghost story in a hushed voice.

"Once upon a time, there was a girl named

Ariel. Her parents had been killed in a car crash, and she was forced to live in an orphanage.

"Now, the head of the orphanage was a woman named Miss Spindly. Miss Spindly had dark eyes and a beak of a nose, and when she came close, Ariel could smell a musty odor, as if Miss Spindly had been tucked away in an attic trunk for years and years . . ."

Gaby watched the faces of the kids surrounding Hank. They were hanging on his every word. When Hank got to the part of the story where Ariel finds a mysterious package outside her door, a few kids shivered and drew back. Hank was really hamming it up, speaking in a low, shivery voice.

"Covering the object was a black cloth that looked like a shroud. Ariel crouched next to the mysterious object and peered under the cloth. Inside was a . . ."

Gaby gasped as cold fingers suddenly gripped her neck. *"Wha . . . ?"* She whirled around. "Lenni! Don't sneak up on me like that!" she said.

"Come on, Gaby," Lenni whispered. "Everybody on the team is going into one of the back rooms. We've got to try Ghostwriter again."

"Okay," Gaby agreed, following her friends as they filed into the small meeting room in the back of the center. She didn't have much hope, but maybe they would manage to reach Ghostwriter this time.

110 The team members sat down at the long table,

and Alex flipped open the casebook again, to the page where he'd written the note to Sam and Emily.

"Come on, Ghostwriter," he whispered. "You've got to come through. We need your help."

"So do Sam and Emily," Casey put in.

The team waited again in silence. Outside in the main room Gaby could hear Hank's hushed voice, and soft moans were coming from the portable stereo.

Suddenly a bloodcurdling scream ripped through the center. Gaby jumped. So did Hector and Lenni.

"Hank must have gotten to a really scary part," Jamal said.

Tina nodded. "I've heard this ghost story before," she said. "What happens is, the girl Ariel gets this present—it's a raven. She doesn't know where it comes from, but it starts talking to her, and—"

Suddenly Casey pointed to the notebook. "Look!" she cried. "It's Ghostwriter!"

Ghostwriter glowed dimly across the page. Gaby struggled to read his message:

October 30, 1938

It was Sam's reply.
Lenni looked at her friends. "We were right," **111**

she said. "Sam and Emily are from 1938, right before World War Two."

The team watched Ghostwriter reading their message about the hoax. Gaby held her breath, afraid to say a word. Everyone else was quiet, too, silently hoping Ghostwriter could get their note back to the past to help Sam and Emily.

The swirling lights grew dimmer and dimmer. Finally they faded completely.

"Come on," Lenni said softly. "Let's get back to the party."

The rest of the team stood up and followed her to the main room.

All they could do now was wait.

October 30, 1938

Sam stared at the door in horror, waiting for it to fly open as the Martians rushed inside.

The descriptions of the creatures from the radio were playing over and over inside his head.

Black eyes that gleam like those of a serpent. A V-shaped mouth with dripping saliva.

Now he was about to come face-to-face with the Martians.

Emily was crying and wheezing, her whole body quaking with terror.

The yellow lights flashed through the window again, forcing Sam to look away toward the book-

case that covered one whole wall of the living room.

Suddenly the letters on the spines of the books began to swirl and dance in the air.

"It's too late, Ghostwriter!" Sam cried out. "The Martians are here! The team can't do anything. . . ."

Then Sam read the message that was floating in the air.

Sam and Emily,
    It's a hoax! The Martians aren't real. You're listening to a story by H. G. Wells, not a news broadcast.

"What?" Sam stared at the words in disbelief. *A hoax?*

Across the room, Emily was sitting up now. She'd read the message, too. "S-S-Sam?" she choked out.

Sam was still trying to piece it together. If the news on the radio was a hoax . . .

A loud banging sounded on the door.

Then who was . . . ?

Before Sam could figure out what was going on, the front door flung open.

"Sam?" a gruff voice called out.

Sam gasped at the tall figure standing in the doorway.

It was Frank! Frank Connor, the chemist who worked at his family's pharmacy. In one hand

Frank held a large flashlight that gave off a strong yellow light. A small parcel was tucked under the other arm.

"You okay?" Frank asked.

Sam lifted a trembling finger and pointed at Emily. "Emily . . ." He couldn't finish the sentence.

Frank took one look at Emily and rushed over to the couch. He ripped open the parcel and pulled out a needle and a vial of medicine. "Here, Emily," he said. He quickly gave her a shot of medicine, then patted her back soothingly. "Take it easy now, honey. The medicine will help your breathing in just a few minutes."

Sam heaved an enormous sigh. He could feel his heart still racing and his whole body was trembling. The Martians were a hoax? He couldn't get over his fright.

Frank sat with Emily for a while longer, waiting for her wheezing to subside. He looked over at Sam and shook his head. "The whole world has gone crazy tonight, Sam," he began. "Right after eight o'clock, people started running into the store saying Martians had landed in Grovers Mill. When your mother heard the news, she tried to call you, but she couldn't get through. Finally I volunteered to come over and check on you two young people."

Sam nodded. "We heard the reports on the radio, and we thought—"

"It's the darnedest thing," Frank continued.

"Everybody said the Martians had declared war, right here in town, but I didn't see a trace of what they were talking about. Except for the roads—they're jammed with traffic. I had to leave my car and come the rest of the way on foot."

Suddenly Emily spoke up. The color had returned to her face, and her breathing sounded almost normal. "I feel much better," she told Sam and Frank. "Thank you for everything."

"You sure scared me, Emily." Sam smiled at his cousin. "After that bottle of medicine broke, I didn't know what to do."

"I'll tell your mother that you're fine," Frank said as he stood up and opened the front door. "She said she'd keep trying to call." Frank stared out into the darkness for a minute, then turned back to Sam. "I don't see a thing out there, except for the moon and a sprinkling of stars. It sure is quiet, for a night when the world's supposed to be coming to an end."

Sam and Emily exchanged looks.

Finally Sam spoke up quietly. "Um, Frank—the whole thing is a big mistake. People thought Martians were invading, but it was just Orson Welles's *Mercury Theatre*. They were broadcasting a story about Martians tonight."

"What?" Frank stared at Sam. "A mistake, you say?"

Sam pointed to the radio. "Turn it on, Frank. See what they're saying now."

Frank clicked on the radio, and the voice of Orson Welles, producer of *Mercury Theatre*, floated over the airways.

Sure enough, he was telling the audience that tonight's broadcast had been based on a work of fiction, *The War of the Worlds*, by H. G. Wells.

"So good-bye, everybody," Orson Welles concluded. "And remember, please . . . if your doorbell rings and nobody's there, that was no Martian . . . it's Halloween."

Frank turned back to Sam, an amazed look on his face. "B-But . . . ," he stammered, "how did you know?"

From across the room, Emily winked at Sam.

Sam grinned, then said to Frank, "Would you believe me if I said that a Halloween ghost told me?"

chapter thirteen

The present, October 30

"Here, Jamal." Gaby pulled down the last of the plastic spiders from the ceiling and tossed it at Jamal.

Jamal threw it into the bag in which he was collecting the decorations. "Come on, Gaby. Let's help Tamara stack up the chairs."

Gaby followed Jamal to the rear of the center. The party had ended a little while ago, and tired trick-or-treaters were still straggling out the door. Judging by the kids' sad faces when it was over, the event had been a big success. Tamara told the team they'd raised a lot of money for the summer program.

Gaby was glad about that but still worried sick about Sam and Emily. Had Ghostwriter gotten the team's message about the hoax to Sam? Gaby was keeping her fingers crossed that he had, and that the news had somehow helped with Emily's asthma attack.

As Gaby walked past a tiny closet along the hallway, she heard a sound. It came again—a low sound, like whimpering.

"Jamal?"

He turned around.

"Did you hear that?" Gaby asked.

He shook his head. "Hear what?"

"That sound," Gaby said. She motioned him over, and this time he heard the noise as well.

"It's coming from inside this closet," Gaby whispered. Cautiously she reached over and turned the doorknob. Jamal stood behind her as she opened the door.

"Oh my gosh," Gaby said when she saw what was inside.

Crouched on the floor next to some empty pails and cleaning supplies was a boy in a pirate costume. He was moaning and sobbing and rubbing his eyes.

"Malcolm!" Jamal exclaimed. "What are you doing here?"

Kevin Clarke's younger brother looked up at them. His nose was running, and tears streamed down his face. "I . . . ran . . . away," he choked out.

"Have you been here all night?" Gaby asked. Malcolm nodded, and she bent down beside him. "It's okay," she said softly.

The little boy stood up and moved into her

open arms. He took a few heaving breaths; then Gaby felt him relax.

"My mom and dad had a big fight on the phone," Malcolm sobbed. "Dad promised to take me and Kevin to L.A., but he never showed up. Then my mother got really mad. She was screaming at him." He looked at Gaby with his big brown eyes. "It was really loud."

"Is that why you ran away?" Jamal asked.

Malcolm nodded. "My mom said that Dad was going to come and get me and take me away from her. I didn't want to go. After Mom went to work, I left. Kevin was in the shower."

Malcolm paused for a second, then said, "I'm really hungry, Gaby. Do you have something to eat? I didn't get any Halloween candy."

Gaby laughed and led the little boy out to the main room, where she found an apple and some juice left over from the snacks Tamara had brought.

"Here, Malcolm," she said. "It's not much, but it's a start. We've got to let your mother know you're—"

Loud, angry voices interrupted Gaby's words.

"What's going on now?" Jamal asked. He headed over to the main doors and opened them. Outside on the steps stood Kevin Clarke. He was shouting angrily at a very tall man dressed in jeans and a black leather jacket.

"I don't believe you, Dad!" Kevin cried. "I   **121**

know you took Malcolm after that fight with Mom. And now you just won't tell me where he is."

Sparks Clarke held up his hands, trying to calm Kevin down. "That's crazy talk, Kevin. I didn't kidnap Malcolm. Why do you think I came down here as soon as I heard your messages on my machine? I was just giving your mother a hard time this morning."

"You're lucky I haven't told Mom about this yet," Kevin went on. "She's going to be so furious . . ."

"Come on, Malcolm," Gaby said softly. She brought the younger boy over to where Kevin stood on the steps. "Hey, Kevin," she called out. "Look who I found."

Kevin was still glaring when he whirled around. His mouth dropped open as he spotted Malcolm standing next to Gaby.

"Malcolm!" he cried. Gaby could see the relief flood over him. "You scared me to death. Where have you been?"

Malcolm hung his head. "I didn't want Dad to take me to live with him," he mumbled, "so I ran away."

Kevin bent down and hugged his little brother. "Were you here all day long?"

Tears dropped from Malcolm's eyes. "No," he said. "First I went to the park, and then I got cold, so I came here. I was hiding in a closet during the

party."

When Gaby glanced over at the boys' father, she saw him shove his hands in his pockets and stare up at one of the streetlights.

Sparks Clarke, the big NBA star, doesn't know what to do, Gaby realized. *Malcolm is his own son, and he hasn't even hugged him or said he was glad to see him.*

Gaby looked over at Jamal. She could tell from the expression on his face that he felt just the way she did: sorry for the Clarke brothers. Obviously, their father wasn't very connected to them.

Finally Sparks Clarke muttered something under his breath about a "nasty custody battle." Then he stalked off into the night.

Wordlessly, Kevin watched his father go. Then he seemed to remember Gaby was there. He looked over at her and gave her a warm smile. "Thanks, Gaby. I was really freaking out about this little guy today."

Gaby smiled back. "No problem," she said.

"Come on, Kevin." Malcolm yanked on his brother's sleeve. "Let's go home. I want a bowl of cereal."

"One minute, Malcolm," Kevin answered. When he looked back at Gaby, he seemed a little unsure of himself. "I wasn't lying about Malcolm, you know. I thought my dad really had kidnapped him."

"I know that now," Gaby said softly.

Kevin looked embarrassed. "I did make up all

that UFO stuff," he mumbled. "I started telling Malcolm stories about aliens and outer space, and then I really got into this TV show about UFO abductions." He shook his head. "It seems stupid now, but at the time, I was having fun telling everyone at school that me and Malcolm got abducted."

"I actually believed you for about two seconds," Gaby said. "Until Alex told me I was crazy."

A few minutes later, Gaby said good night and watched the brothers head off down the street. They had nearly reached the end of the block when Gaby yelled out, "Hey, Kevin!"

He turned around to face her.

"You're a really good brother," she said.

"I know!" Kevin yelled back. "Malcolm's lucky to have me for his main man."

For the first time in days, Gaby was sure Kevin Clarke was telling the truth.

An hour later, Gaby dropped down on a couch next to Lenni in the community center. The team had finally finished cleaning up, and now they were getting ready to lock up and go home.

"I'm so tired," Gaby said. "And worried," she added. "Almost three hours have gone by since we heard from Ghostwriter."

"I can't stand not knowing about Sam and Emily," Tina agreed. "What if—"

Suddenly Gaby noticed letters on a poster swirling. "All right!" she cheered softly.

The team looked up, where letters were dancing in the air.

Congratulations, Team!

"That must mean Sam and Emily are okay." Tina let out a breath.

Lenni pulled out her pen and wrote a note to Ghostwriter. "Did Sam get our message? Is Emily okay?"

I'll be right back, Ghostwriter promised.

A few minutes later, he returned with a message from Sam.

Dear Team,

Thank you for everything! Emily and I thought the end of the world had come until we got your message about the broadcast. You'll be glad to know that she got her medicine in time, too.

The team read Sam's words and quickly replied, "You're welcome. We're so glad Emily's okay."

I just want to know one more thing, Sam wrote back a few minutes later. How were you able to figure out that the War of the Worlds wasn't real?

As the team read Sam's note, Hector reminded them that they couldn't let Ghostwriter travel back and forth much longer. It had been a long night, and his powers probably wouldn't last.

"We're from the future," Lenni wrote back. "That's how we knew."

Beneath that note, she added a special message, just for Ghostwriter. "Happy Halloween to our friend the ghost."

BOO! Ghostwriter wrote back, then disappeared into the past.

October 31, 1938

Sam lay in bed with his journal open on his lap. When his mother had finally arrived home from work at midnight, she'd helped him into bed and made Emily comfortable out on the couch. Now Sam could hear his cousin's snores drifting through the quiet house. He guessed his mother was asleep, too.

But Sam was wide awake, talking with Ghostwriter and the team. Now he was waiting to find out how they'd known about the hoax.

A few minutes later, Ghostwriter returned with an answer to his question.

We're from the future. That's how we knew.

What? Sam blinked in surprise at the message from his new friends. The team was from the future? That's how they'd known that the broadcast was just a Halloween prank?

All this time, Sam had thought they were from a nearby town, or maybe even from Grovers Mill. He'd never for a second imagined they were from the future.

Jeepers! Sam thought. *If the team is from the future, then they can probably tell me which team will win the pennant in the World Series next year. Or if things will ever get any easier for Mom.*

They might even know what will happen in Europe. . . . Will war really break out? Will Hitler keep trying to take over countries like Poland and Czechoslovakia?

Sam reached for his pen, trying to decide which question to ask first. Ghostwriter glowed dimly across the page, reminding Sam that his friend was waiting.

And then Sam changed his mind. He didn't know Ghostwriter very well, but he'd learned enough about him to see that he was tired. The ghost had done enough traveling in time for today.

"Thank you for your help with the Martains, Ghostwriter," Sam wrote finally. "I hope you can rest now."

You're welcome, Sam. By the way, your mother's right—you do need to improve your spelling. It's M<u>a</u>rt<u>ia</u>ns, not M<u>a</u>rt<u>ai</u>ns.

Sam smiled sheepishly as he watched the lights shimmering across the page.

So long, Sam, Ghostwriter wrote. Enjoy life's mysteries.

And then the ghost was gone for good.

Reluctantly Sam closed his journal and placed it on his nightstand.

What a night, he thought. He'd met aliens that were made up, and a ghost that was real! And he'd met a group of kids from the future! And to think he'd told his mother his life was too boring to write about. He had been completely wrong.

Sam stared out his bedroom window at the dark, starry sky. In the distance he could make out the Big Dipper, glowing brightly among all the other stars.

Who knows? Sam thought as he closed his eyes. *Tonight was a false alarm, but maybe life does exist somewhere out there.*

The present, October 30

It was nearly midnight when the team left the Fort Greene Community Center.

Witching hour, Gaby thought. She paused on the steps as Jamal closed the door behind them, then locked it with Tamara's keys. As she looked at her friends still in their costumes, she couldn't help thinking what a strange day it had been.

Lenni seemed to be having similar thoughts. "Isn't it weird," she began, "that we didn't believe

Kevin Clarke tonight and he was telling the truth?"

"And that we thought Martians really had invaded New Jersey, but it turned out to be a made-up story," Hector added.

Gaby nodded, suddenly remembering the fortune tucked away in her pocket. *Things are not what they seem,* she thought. Just as her English teacher had pointed out, sometimes it *was* hard to tell truth from lies, fact from fiction.

Hector and Lenni hurried down the steps to the sidewalk. But Gaby lingered for a minute, gazing up at the immense sky over her head. The clouds had drifted away, leaving behind hundreds of twinkling stars. Gaby could even make out the Big Dipper nestled among the other constellations.

"I don't care if Kevin Clarke was making up the UFO abduction story," Casey suddenly whispered into Gaby's ear. She was standing beside Gaby at the top of the steps. "I really believe aliens exist. Maybe someday I'll even get to meet one for myself," she added.

Gaby was about to tell her friend that it was silly to believe that when something made her change her mind—the sight of the immense sky stretched out over her head. Tonight it seemed so dark and mysterious.

Who knows what's really out there? Gaby thought. "Maybe the aliens *will* visit you, Casey," she whispered back.

"Hey, Witch Gabriela," Alex called out from the bottom of the steps. "Come on. It's late."

"I'm coming, I'm coming," Gaby told him.

And then she and Casey headed back down toward Earth, where their friends stood waiting.

If you enjoyed *Alien Alert,* you'll also enjoy this exciting Ghostwriter book!

THE MAN WHO VANISHED

by Amy Keyishian

A horror author may have come to a horrifying end! Alex and Tina can't wait to meet writer Emory Rex. But before they get the chance, Rex vanishes from the middle of a packed horror convention. The rest of the Ghostwriter Team must pitch in and help their friends find the missing author. Using clues from his own books, the team starts closing in on Rex—and running into some frighteningly weird suspects! If the team doesn't find the writer, they'll never know how his latest scary story ends. . . .